Praise for *The Secret of Dr*

★ "A captivating and suspenseful tale of the power of female friendship and the pain of growing up . . . Heart-rending and genuine, this magical coming-of-age story is not to be missed."

—*Kirkus Reviews*, starred review

★ "The inclusion of diverse characters enhances [this] . . . thoughtful, atmospheric fairy tale."

—*School Library Journal*, starred review

"This book is wise and wonderful."

—William Alexander,
National Book Award–winning author
of *Goblin Secrets*

"Mesmerizing . . . This is an adventure story, yes, but it is something more—it is a story of the transformational power of curiosity, tenacity, and courage."

—Kelly Barnhill, author of *The Witch's Boy*

"The Carse is a dark, foreboding place within a creepily blissful land. Like Aon and Jeniah, I felt myself drawn there . . . A compelling examination of what it means to be sad while finding unexpected happiness."

—Sarah Prineas, author of the Magic Thief series

"Part fairy tale, part seemingly utopian society with a dark underbelly, this is a gripping, compelling story." —*Booklist*

"Delightful . . . This reminded me quite a bit of classic works by Ursula K. Le Guin and Madeleine L'Engle."
—Kiera Parrott, LibraryJournal.com

"An exciting fairytale that unfolds itself in a variety of delightful layers as the story progresses . . . I am simply in awe of Farrey." —*Forever Lost in Literature*

"Inventive fairy tale world-building."
—*Publishers Weekly*

"If you are looking for a book to get your child away from all the technology and get lost in the world of words, look no further. *The Secret of Dreadwillow Carse* has everything one needs to get lost in the magic." —*Geeks of Doom*

Named to *Kirkus Reviews'* Best Books of 2016

The Secret of Dreadwillow Carse

The Secret of DREADWILLOW CARSE

Brian Farrey

Algonquin Young Readers 2017

Published by
Algonquin Young Readers
an imprint of Algonquin Books of Chapel Hill
Post Office Box 2225
Chapel Hill, North Carolina 27515-2225

a division of
Workman Publishing
225 Varick Street
New York, New York 10014

First paperback edition, Algonquin Young Readers, May 2017. Originally published in hardcover by Algonquin Young Readers in April 2016.
Printed in the United States of America.
Published simultaneously in Canada by
Thomas Allen & Son Limited.
Design by Carla Weise.

LIBRARY OF CONGRESS CATALOGING-IN-PUBLICATION DATA
Names: Farrey, Brian, author.
Title: The secret of Dreadwillow Carse / Brian Farrey.
Description: First edition. | Chapel Hill, North Carolina : Algonquin Young Readers, 2016. | Summary: A princess and a peasant girl, who hides a sorrow in a town where everyone lives with unending joy, embark on a dangerous quest to outwit a centuries-old warning foretelling the fall of the Monarchy.
Identifiers: LCCN 2015031467 | ISBN 9781616205058 (HC)
Subjects: | CYAC: Fairy tales. | Princesses—Fiction. | Kings, queens, rulers, etc.—Fiction. | Friendship—Fiction. | Depression, Mental—Fiction.
Classification: LCC PZ8.F25 Se 2016 | DDC [Fic]—dc23
LC record available at http://lccn.loc.gov/2015031467

ISBN 978-1-61620-697-0 (PB)

10 9 8 7 6 5 4 3 2 1

First Paperback Edition

FOR MY NIECES:

Never stop asking "why?"

AND FOR KATE:

I borrowed your D&D character's name.

Hope that's okay.

The Secret of DREADWILLOW CARSE

Chapter One

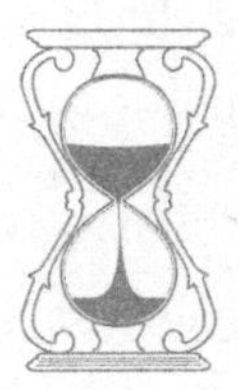

THE QUEEN WAS DYING. THIS MUCH WAS CERTAIN.

Healers from all parts of the Monarchy had gathered in Nine Towers to examine Her Majesty. For weeks, the halls of the royal palace echoed with their discussions. Everyone had a different theory about the nature of the illness that gripped Queen Sula. In the end, they could agree on only these two facts:

There was no cure.

A month more was as long as anyone dared hope she would live.

It was not unusual for monarchs to take ill and die relatively young. It had, in fact, been the case for as long as anyone could remember. But there had always been a plan. When Jeniah, the queen's daughter, turned eighteen, her mother would abdicate and allow the princess to ascend to the throne. That was how it had always worked, for the nearly one thousand years their family had ruled.

But Jeniah had just turned twelve. And if the healers were to be believed, she would ascend to power much sooner than planned.

When word spread of the queen's fate, Jeniah locked herself in her bedchambers for three days. No one disturbed her. The servants who'd helped raise the young princess left trays of food near her door so she wouldn't starve. But no one spoke to the heir apparent. It was impossible to understand what the girl felt.

Jeniah sat in her room, refusing to cry. She braided her long, black hair with green glass beads. She played her recorder, filling the room with a lullaby her mother had taught her. But she would not cry. She knew the tears would come—and that they would be unstoppable—once her mother was truly gone. Knowing death was coming for the queen didn't make Jeniah sad. She was too terrified to be sad.

Jeniah knew nothing about *being* a queen. She had

never been permitted in the throne room when her mother held court. "The time will come for all that," the princess's caregivers had promised each time Jeniah asked to watch. "Someday." Everyone had believed Jeniah had six more years to learn.

But "someday" turned out to be "now." She wasn't ready. She was scared she wouldn't have time. Surely there was much to learn about being a fair and just leader.

Jeniah had to turn her terror into resolve. She *would* learn how to be a queen. The time for tears would come. For now, she had to stay strong. She stared in the mirror, shook her finger at her reflection, and reminded herself to be brave.

So, when the queen knocked softly on Jeniah's bedroom door at the end of the princess's third day of seclusion and whispered for her daughter, the young girl answered with squared shoulders and a straight back. "You should be in bed," she told her mother. Her words sounded braver than she felt. For months, Jeniah had watched her mother's health dwindle away.

The woman who stood at her door was barely recognizable as the one who'd raised her. The queen's illness made her appear much older than she truly was. Her eyes were swollen; her back was hunched. Where mother and daughter once shared smooth, dark skin, the queen's was now dry and cracked. Despite all that, Jeniah didn't have to search hard to find the kindness she'd always seen in her mother's regal face.

"Come," the queen said, her voice wavering. "We're going to the top of Lithe Tower."

As she took her mother's arm, Jeniah's breath seized. Lithe Tower was the tallest of the castle's nine monoliths, twice the size of the others. It was the highest point in all the land, with a view reserved for the monarch. The only exception occurred when an heir apparent was escorted there shortly before the start of a new reign.

This truth—this hard, hard truth—weakened Jeniah's march up to the tower entrance. Her knees trembled. *This is real*, she told herself. For the three days she'd locked herself in her room, her mother's illness had not been real.

Jeniah and the queen strode arm in arm down a narrow passage made of rough, silver-dappled stone. As they came to a wooden door at the hall's end, the queen produced a long key. It had teeth in four directions, like a weather vane.

"Bring the torch," Queen Sula instructed as the lock on the door clicked open. Jeniah took a torch from the wall. Together, they crossed the door's threshold. The spiral staircase beyond was so narrow, they had to proceed single file. They climbed and climbed the endless stairs. The princess moved closer to her mother, where the scent of the rose water and mint salve that eased the queen's pain overpowered the passageway's musty smell.

The queen struggled with each step, keeping one hand on the wall. Despite this, Jeniah imagined that the shadows cowered from her mother's approach the farther up they went.

As Jeniah's legs started to ache, the stairs disappeared into an opening in the ceiling. Queen and princess emerged from the dark stairwell onto the very top of Lithe Tower. They stood on a wide, flat stone circle covered by a clear glass dome. When Jeniah moved to the edge and looked down, she could see the eight other cloud-colored spires that made up the rest of Nine Towers forming a circle around Lithe. Not far from the castle gates, a slender dirt road split the countryside on its way to the nearest town, Emberfell.

"Look around," the queen said.

Jeniah stepped back. Nothing blocked her view. The Caprack Mountains on the horizon joined land

and sky like jagged gray stitches. That one seam kept the pair united in all directions.

Her gaze swept down from the skyline. Rolling fields, lush green forests, and verdant farmland rich with golden harvests stretched out from the base of Nine Towers. A twisting river cut a swath through the west lands, looking like liquid fire in the setting sun. As dusk approached, lanterns from a patchwork of towns and villages made a pinprick mosaic of light across the land.

It was the most beautiful thing Jeniah had ever seen.

"This is our Monarchy," Queen Sula said. "It has been a land of peace and prosperity for a thousand years. Your first duty as queen is, and always will be, to protect that."

Jeniah nodded. Standing in place, she turned around slowly. She memorized every inch of the land, as if sealing the promise to serve as guardian. As she did, something curious happened. The tiny dots of warm, amber light that marked every village and town for miles flickered and, one by one, turned bright blue. She turned to her mother, eyebrow raised.

The queen smiled. "Tonight is what the people call Tower Rise. It's a rare holiday. It occurs only when a new monarch ascends Lithe Tower for the first time."

The queen held up her right hand where she wore two identical rings, each with an opal wrapped in silver filigree. Only the monarch could wear these. Queen Sula slid one ring from her own finger onto Jeniah's. "The people know you're here, watching over them. They know you are no longer merely a princess. You are now Queen Ascendant. This is their tribute."

Jeniah closed her fist. The ring hung so loosely on her finger, she was afraid it would slip off. In the distance, the blue lights winked as if the entire Monarchy were showing approval. Jeniah imagined she should have felt honored by the people's gesture, but instead she felt embarrassed, as if she'd been caught spying. Still, she continued to survey all that would soon be hers to govern. Her eyes fell just east of the river and stopped.

Between the rushing river and a thriving forest sat a small patch of land, a blemish scarring the middle of the otherwise gorgeous realm. Jeniah had almost missed it. Even now, as she tried to look directly at it, she found it difficult. Almost as if her eyes *didn't want* to see it.

Determined, she moved to a brass spyglass mounted in a Y-shaped stone at the platform's edge. She trained the glass's lens on the dark area. Black trees with black branches and black leaves grappled with one another in an eternal choke hold. Shadows seemed drawn to the unsightly region—a serrated slash shaped like the curved blade Cook used to butcher cows. No light could touch it.

Or maybe light *refused* to touch it.

The queen laid a hand on the princess's shoulder. "Do you know what that is?"

Jeniah knew. Her heart had told her, the moment her eyes fell on the spot. "Dreadwillow Carse." The words thrummed on her lips. For as long as Jeniah could remember, the name had only ever lived as a whisper among the royal family's servants. A footnote in the lectures of her teachers. An oddity—like a treasonous, distant relative—that was never, ever discussed.

"And what do you know about it?" the queen asked.

Never, ever discussed, save one fact that had been repeated to her over and over since Jeniah could first talk. "I'm not to go there. Ever."

"Very good," the queen said. "Wherever you go in the Monarchy, you will be welcomed warmly. But you must never set foot in Dreadwillow Carse."

Jeniah, who'd never been good at holding in the thoughts that pressed against her insides, asked the necessary question. "Why?"

The queen stood as tall as her illness would allow. "It is forbidden. The people rely on us to maintain peace and prosperity. And it is written in the oldest books: if any monarch enters Dreadwillow Carse, then the Monarchy will fall."

A chill crawled on spider's legs over Jeniah's hands. She'd been told before never to enter. She'd never been told the Monarchy was at stake. "Do you understand?" the queen asked.

Jeniah knew that tone. It meant the queen wasn't to be questioned. Yet it was a tone that always *inspired* questions in Jeniah. "But why—?"

"You can never go to Dreadwillow Carse," the queen interrupted. And then she repeated, "Do you understand?"

"Yes, Mother. I understand."

But Jeniah didn't understand. Each step she took as they descended the crooked stairs fanned the flames of new questions for which she *needed* answers.

What was Dreadwillow Carse? How was it possible they did not rule there? And, most important, why would the Monarchy end if she entered the Carse?

When they returned to the castle halls, the queen's gait faltered. Jeniah took her mother's arm and guided her back to her bedchambers.

"Time is short," the queen said. "Tomorrow, you will meet with a new tutor. He will teach you what you need to know to rule over your people justly. Listen to everything he says."

"Yes, Mother."

The queen laced her fingers with her daughter's. "You will make an excellent queen."

THAT NIGHT, LYING in bed, Jeniah tried to think about how badly she wanted to make her mother proud by upholding the legacy of benevolence laid out by her ancestors. She tried to think about how the lives and happiness of everyone in the Monarchy depended on her learning to become a fair and just queen. She tried to think about anything and everything that wasn't Dreadwillow Carse.

If any monarch enters Dreadwillow Carse, then the Monarchy will fall.

She failed.

Chapter Two

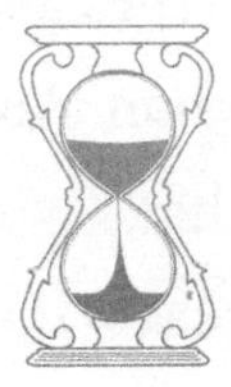

THE QUEEN WAS DYING AND EVERYONE KNEW IT.

But as usual, nothing had changed.

Aon Greenlaw sat on a rock at the western border of Emberfell. She stared at her hometown, where revelry filled the streets. Everywhere she looked, people danced and sang merrily to the reels played by the musicians stationed at every corner. Colorful silk banners zigzagged from rooftop to rooftop. Even here, at the farthest edge of town, she could smell the freshly baked cream puffs that the village bakery made only for special occasions.

Special? Aon thought. *It's not right*. This was something

Aon thought often. But she only ever *thought* it. Saying that—or anything like it—would prompt her father to repeat the same thing he always said.

"The queen wants her people to be happy," he would say, and then he'd playfully trace a star on her cheek, connecting her freckles with his finger. That was all anyone said when Aon questioned the joy that filled the land. "That's what every monarch has wanted for a thousand years. It would be disrespectful not to honor their wishes."

And although Aon was told this anytime someone died, or poor weather ended a picnic, or she had any reason to possibly be sad, she had a hard time believing that anyone—queen or not—would want people to be happy that she was dying.

Three days earlier, when she'd first heard of the queen's illness, Aon had gone to bed. She'd pretended to have the flu, but really, she was sick with grief. The queen had always been good. She didn't deserve to die. And then there was Princess Jeniah, only a month older than Aon. What would it be like to rule the Monarchy at this age? How must the princess have been feeling?

But Aon kept these questions to herself. She had no choice. The Monarchy had always been a rich and thriving land and its people a happy and peaceful populace. She'd learned long ago not to express melancholy or even discuss it. To admit to anyone that she was sad about the queen would mean admitting the very worst thing about herself, the thing she never wanted anyone to know.

That deep, deep down, in ways she couldn't understand, Aon was broken.

She *wanted* to be happy all the time like everyone else. She wanted to give in to bliss and rest in the knowledge that their monarch kept them all safe and prosperous. But while Aon could fool everyone else into thinking she was just like them, she would never be able to fool herself.

So, all day long, as Emberfell prepared to celebrate Tower Rise, Aon had played her part. She'd thrown herself into the merriment. She'd danced joyously. She'd laughed as her neighbor friends wove her long, blond hair into a braid that circled her head. She'd appeared, for all to see, thoroughly and unquestionably happy. Until at last, as the sun started to set and the excitement in Emberfell hit a fever pitch, she seized her chance and quietly slipped away. She took the western path to the one place where she felt whole and well and normal.

With her back to the town, Aon took a deep breath and stared into the maw of Dreadwillow Carse.

In all other directions, the edges of the village gently faded into the picturesque landscapes beyond. Brown earth gave way to green grass and thick trees. The change was so gentle, it was hard to tell where Emberfell ended and the world beyond began.

But along the west side, which butted up against the black marsh, there was no mistaking where the village stopped. A pronounced dark line marked Emberfell's border, as if the ground had been scorched by an invisible wall of flame.

From an early age, all in Emberfell were advised to stay away from the Carse. The warning was scarcely needed. One look into the unforgiving blackness sent unwary travelers scurrying. Most in Emberfell saw the Carse as a blight to be endured.

Aon saw it as something else: a remedy.

Clutching a long, unlit candle in her sweaty hand, she inched forward. Her toes just grazed the black border. A tingly mix of excitement and fear buzzed through her. The terrifying thrill of standing at the edge of a cliff, the dizziness of climbing the tallest hill, and the pain of a deep wound that felt like it could never be healed all wrestled inside her. And eagerness. Aon also felt eager.

Everything—the hair on the back of her neck, the knot in the pit of her stomach—*begged* Aon not to move forward. The Carse had this effect on anyone who passed by. But Aon wasn't like anyone else. She alone could ignore that feeling. She lit the candle and walked cautiously onto the black ground beyond.

One . . . two . . . three . . . She counted the steps in her head like always.

The earth in Dreadwillow Carse gave slightly. The moist soil rushed in to meet her feet and crept up the edges of her boots. She trod softly, fearing her steps would convince the mire to swallow her whole.

Thirteen . . . fourteen . . . fifteen . . .

With each step, a weight pulled at Aon's shoulders, like the heavy wool cerements the people of Emberfell wrapped around the dead. Something slick and thorny took purchase in her chest. The sadness she felt over the queen consumed her, drowning out Emberfell's raucous celebration in the distance.

Twenty-one . . . twenty-two . . . twenty-three . . . Aon paused as something slithered at her ankles. A tangle of mirebramble, the carnivorous vines known for pulling anything that moved down into the Carse's muck, froze near her heels. She pressed her tongue against the back of her teeth impatiently. When she refused to move, the vines slid off in search of other prey. Aon continued.

Twenty-four . . . twenty-five . . . twenty-six . . . The farthest she'd ever gone before was thirty-two steps. But today she needed to go farther. She *needed* to.

Today is the day, she promised herself as she had so many times before. *Today I learn what* really *happened to Mother.*

A hint of something rank—spoiled milk maybe?—hung in the air. Dreadwillow trees lined the path, their branches with teardrop-shaped leaves drooping under the burden of festering, black moss. They brushed Aon's shoulders as she passed beneath. Each touch sapped her of hope and convinced her she'd never leave.

What a change it was to shrug off the burden of joy! At home, she had all the food she could ever want, comforts that would be lavish and shameful were they not afforded to everyone in the land. Every monarch had seen to it that the people wanted for nothing and suffered no indignities.

Yet it was here, giving in to her worry and sorrow,

where Aon felt less broken. No one would understand her sadness. She could not understand their glee.

Aon stopped at a hook-shaped rock that poked up out of the ground. In all her previous visits to the Carse, she'd never gone farther than this. She'd never been able to. Here, at this spot, she was filled with alarm and exhaustion. *Just a few more steps*, she coaxed herself. But her legs failed to obey. Resigned, Aon closed her eyes and listened. After several moments of silence, she heard it.

There were no words. Just a light tune that trilled from somewhere in the darkest depths of the Carse. A sad, haunting waltz. It was almost like singing. But it couldn't be. No one lived here. A trick of the wind in the trees, she'd always told herself.

Aon let her head roll back and her arms hang limply at her sides. When she heard that song, she felt as if she'd been turned into a stream. She wanted just to stand there and pour herself into the song, itself a melodic river. They would fill each other.

A viscous mist rose off the dark-watered bog on either side of her path. The giddiness Aon felt at being able to express her sadness vanished, replaced swiftly by terror. This always happened. The longer she stayed inside the Carse, the sorrow turned to fear.

The comfort she found in the strange music failed her. Now the music sounded shrill and discordant. She turned and hurried back out of the swamp.

As she stepped across the border onto the path outside Emberfell, Aon's misery melted away. Her mind cleared. As always, the haunting dirge vanished. A pang hiccupped inside her, and she felt as if something very, very valuable had been ripped from her head. Or her heart.

She took three deep breaths. Each inhalation brought her calm; each exhalation took away a little more terror. In moments, she went back to being who she believed she was: a slightly broken girl.

A chorus of bells rang out. Aon shot a glance at Emberfell. Almost immediately, the dancing and merriment stopped as the whole town scrambled about. It was later than she thought. Wiping away any telltale tears, Aon wended her way through the town and headed for the village's east side. Outside the mayor's house, she tapped the base of the tall glass statue of Queen Sula that watched over Emberfell with arms extended, welcoming all. Everyone who passed the statue touched the base for luck and made a wish. Aon always wished not to be caught going into the Carse.

Turning onto the street where she lived, Aon could

just make out the outline of her father. He was leaning on his crutch in front of their house at the end of the lane.

Aon's father hobbled forward, holding a small tin lantern. The fire within cast shadows like cobwebs across his jovial face. As he reached out to hug his daughter, he nearly fell. Aon chided him gently. "You should be sitting."

Her father pointed up and down the street. All the town's families stood outside their homes, holding lanterns. "If I sit, I can't hold it high enough for our new queen to see. And we don't want that, do we?"

Aon kissed her father's hand. No one, she often thought, loved the Monarchy more than her father. He would do anything to please his queen.

The cry of a horn echoed down the streets of Emberfell. "It's time," Father said.

Aon bent over and picked up a cube of blue glass at her father's feet. For days, he had collected scraps of broken glass. He'd made the cube using tree sap to bind the pieces together and shield the sharp edges. When the horn sounded again, Aon slid the cube over the lantern. Father lifted it high over his head. Everyone in Emberfell placed similar domes of blue glass over their lights. The village immediately got darker.

A cheer rang out from the crowd. Aon turned her gaze southwest. Nine Towers had become a distant silhouette. The queen and the princess were no doubt at the very top of Lithe Tower.

Aon stared into their lantern. While everyone else's light shone a solid blue, her father's cube twinkled with dozens of azures and sapphires and cobalts, and more blues than she could count. It didn't burn the brightest, but it was certainly the most beautiful.

"So?" Father asked. "Do you think Princess Jeniah will be happy?"

Aon wondered, as she often did, if her father ever suspected. Could he squint at her, even now in the dim light, and see not his daughter but an ungrateful girl with imperfect joy? She believed that if he could, she might go to Dreadwillow Carse and never return. The shame would be that terrible.

Aon smiled, because she knew she was supposed to, and she squeezed her father's hand. "Aren't we all?"

Chapter Three

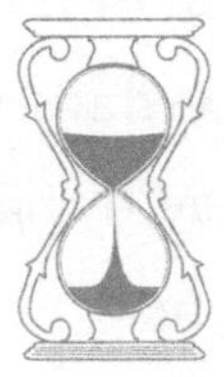

THE LIBRARY THAT TOOK UP THE MAJORITY OF SORIN TOWER WAS said to be the finest in the land. Some of the servants joked that there were so many books in the library, the queen could have used them to build a tenth tower. It was here that the sum of all the Monarchy's knowledge was kept. It was also here that Jeniah had resolved to discover the secret of Dreadwillow Carse. Arms shaking under the weight of the books she'd gathered, the princess wove her way through the stacks. She scanned the spines, searching for any titles that could help in her quest.

The History of Napkin Folding? No. *A Compendium of Tax Tables*? Definitely not.

Making her way toward her favorite table—the one near the stained-glass window with an image of one of her ancestors, King Isaar—Jeniah paused to glance at the library's collection of fairy tales. She smiled to herself. She missed the days when her mother had taught her their language by having Jeniah read her a story each night before bed.

Some children read storybooks and dreamt of being princesses and princes. In those stories, royalty was often brave. They took journeys that made them the heroes the people of the land needed. But a real princess or prince would read the same books and think, *My life's not like that at all*.

So what did princesses dream of?

For Jeniah, it was magic.

Tales of powerful wizards casting spells had captured her imagination from a young age. From the moment she first knew she would be queen one day, Jeniah hoped to discover that magic really was possible. Then, she wouldn't *need* to know how to rule. Magic would mean she would always do what was right.

But Jeniah had been raised to believe that magic

was a lie. *A clever fiction*, her last tutor, Miss Dellers, had called it. *An illusion that beguiles even as it burns.*

And it wasn't only Miss Dellers. Over the years, Jeniah had been instructed by seven different tutors—all exemplary scholars in their fields—and they'd all said the same thing. No matter the lesson—and the subject matters ranged from etiquette to advanced mathematics—the conversation almost always turned to the idea of magic. Jeniah made sure of that.

But the scholars all agreed. Magic was a lovely idea and nothing more.

And yet . . .

Of all the questions that fought for attention in Jeniah's mind following her trip up Lithe Tower, the most powerful proved to be this: What could possibly topple the entire Monarchy should a monarch step a single foot inside the Carse?

Magic. That had to be it.

If there was magic in her Monarchy—or the Carse—then Jeniah needed to know about it. Magic, she felt, would make her a great queen. And maybe, just maybe, it could save her mother.

Jeniah had known about the Carse all her life. It had never been more than a fable to her, a scary story the royals told one another on the darkest of nights. But even though curiosity ran through Jeniah as if it were her very blood, she'd never before felt the need to learn more about the desolate place. That had changed. Why?

Because last night, she had *seen* it.

The Carse, the warning . . . They had only ever been words. Now, it was all real. Now, there were *consequences*. Now, the sight of the twisted, black, and impenetrable bog burned in Jeniah's memory. Each time the image invaded her thoughts, questions—like flaming arrows in the night—accompanied it.

Every future monarch had first been taken to Lithe Tower, just as Jeniah had. Been shown the Monarchy, as she had. And, no doubt, been reminded never to enter Dreadwillow Carse. And for more than a thousand years, the Monarchy had endured and thrived. Each monarch had obeyed.

Yet since seeing the Carse, Jeniah had been unable to stop the deluge of questions that occupied her thoughts. This vexed the princess. Questions without ready answers were new to Jeniah. Growing up, she'd had very little to wonder about. From an early age, she had been spoon-fed all she needed to know. If her mother told her something, it was true. A queen was not to be disputed. If a tutor taught Jeniah history, she could rely on the account, as her mother had chosen the tutor.

So, it was very strange for Jeniah to suddenly find her brain exploding with queries and quandaries and the notion that there were things to know that weren't just going to be imparted to her, as had been her experience. Things she *shouldn't* know . . . but felt she *needed* to.

Where had the decree come from? Had anyone ever questioned it? Were others' inquiries as swiftly silenced as Jeniah's had been? Had any of her ancestors, stalwart and beloved leaders to the last, ever *tried* to learn more? Had Jeniah's mother, who had never accepted any answer she didn't like, ever once sought the truth?

Jeniah had tried to shake off her doubts. She'd promised her mother she would never go to Dreadwillow Carse. That was what it took to be queen. But ignoring questions didn't banish them. She knew there was only one thing to cure this sickness of curiosity. Just one sure tonic.

Answers.

So, that morning, she'd thrown herself into the books. She'd climbed countless stairs, visiting each of Sorin Tower's twenty floors to recover the dustiest, most ancient tomes the mammoth library held. She'd curled up in different corners, resting books on her raised knees, and struggled to translate forgotten languages she barely recognized. She'd pored over ancient scrolls so brittle and faded, she hadn't dared sneeze and risk scattering them to dust. In everything she'd read thus far, in everything she'd learned, only one fact seemed to hold true.

The Carse didn't exist.

Not officially, anyway. No history revealed its origin. No royal biography mentioned its significance. In all, Jeniah examined nearly eighty texts—some rumored to be as old as the land itself—and only three mentioned the Carse. Those three tomes told her what she already knew: *if any monarch enters Dreadwillow Carse, then the Monarchy will fall.*

Exhausted after hours of reading, Jeniah slumped over a table. She'd just closed her bleary eyes when a thunderous crack announced the opening of the library door. She looked up, startled. She'd asked the servants not to disturb her. So who would possibly . . . ?

A short, round man with sickly pale skin bounded into the room. The princess blinked at the sight. The man wore ratty old furs tied to him with frayed bits of rope. Jeniah almost couldn't see his face for the salt-and-pepper hair that engulfed his head. His bare feet were coated in an inch of oily black mud that squished with every step he took. A weathered leather glove covered most of his outstretched left forearm. A sleek falcon with feathers that matched the man's hair color gripped the glove with shiny white talons.

Was this . . . ? It couldn't be.

In her drive to learn all she could about the Carse, Jeniah had forgotten about the new tutor her mother had promised. And even if she had remembered to expect him, nothing could have prepared her to expect . . . *this*.

The man, who had a distinct waddle when he walked, stopped next to Jeniah. A strong odor of lavender and sulfur hovered about him. He smiled broadly, revealing crooked teeth, one of which was framed with a thin strip of gold. "You must be Jeniah."

The princess's eyes narrowed. Typically, anyone who approached her did so with a bow. Called her "Your Highness." At the very least, referred to her as *Princess* Jeniah. She'd never really liked the formality. But its absence was peculiar.

The man flicked his wrist. The falcon cawed, flew into the air, and perched atop the nearest bookcase. "I believe you're expecting me."

No, the princess thought. *No, I really wasn't*. But she nodded hesitantly. "You're my new tutor."

When the man squinted at this, his eyebrows swallowed his eyes. "If you like."

Jeniah started to wonder if an intruder had entered the castle. Her past teachers had worn the long, flowing robes of a scholar. They'd carried sacks full of books, assorted quills, and dioramas depicting key events in the history of the Monarchy. This man had nothing. Except his glove. And the bird.

"I don't believe," she said, eyeing the falcon above, "that animals are allowed in the library."

"And why not?" the man demanded, scratching his thick beard. "Gerheart up there? He has as much right to learn as anyone."

"But he can't read."

"Reading," the man said, pulling up a chair, "is just *one* way of learning. For example, my name is Skonas. There, you learned something by hearing. True?"

Jeniah found herself gripping the sides of her chair tightly. What sort of tutor was this? "My mother said you would teach me how to be queen," she said, sitting up straight.

"Did she? I don't recall that being in the job description."

"Well, then why are you here?"

Skonas rubbed his hands together. "I am here to teach you three lessons. You will then use those lessons to set yourself a fourth and final lesson."

"And . . . and then I'll know how to be queen?"

Skonas sniffed. "Is that important?"

Jeniah's heart fell. He wasn't making any sense. This odd man did not seem capable of teaching her anything, let alone how to rule her people. Clearly the queen, in her weakened state, had not been very diligent in choosing her daughter's new tutor.

"This is your first lesson. It's—" Skonas paused as Jeniah scrambled to take out a piece of parchment and dip her quill in an inkwell. He gave her the most curious look, as if he had no idea what she was doing. Then he turned his back and continued. "It's the lesson from which all other lessons spring: you are your own best teacher. Repeat that."

Jeniah's brow furrowed, but she obeyed. "I am my own best teacher."

Skonas spun around. "Do you believe that?"

"Do I believe what?"

"That you are your own best teacher."

Jeniah looked down at the parchment and quill. She found herself longing for Miss Dellers. Things were much clearer with the stately woman. Miss Dellers spoke only to impart important knowledge. Jeniah had no idea if any of what Skonas was saying was worth writing down.

"If that were true," she said slowly, "you'd be out of a job. Wouldn't you?"

Skonas cackled. "Very astute," he said. "Strangely clever. You're beginning well." But he didn't answer her question.

Sighing, she dipped her quill into the inkwell again. But before she could write a single word, Skonas snatched her parchment away.

"What are you doing?" he asked, holding the page at arm's length as if it were poisonous.

"I'm writing that down. I write down all my lessons. And if all other lessons come from the first lesson," Jeniah reasoned, "it must be the most important."

Skonas looked amused. "Yes, I can see why you'd think that."

"So it's true?"

"No."

Skonas crumpled up the parchment and tossed it aside. Jeniah balled her fists.

"No," the teacher repeated, "it is not the most important lesson. The most important is the fourth. And when we get to that point—*if* we get to that point—there will be no need to write it down."

Jeniah tossed her quill aside, exasperated. "And why is that?"

Skonas paused. Then he leaned forward and looked deeply into the girl's eyes. The princess felt her pulse pound in her throat. She'd already resolved to dismiss everything the man had said. But that look in his eyes . . . The same instinct that fueled her curiosity about Dreadwillow Carse now told her one thing: Skonas was about to speak an irrefutable truth.

"Because it will be imprinted on your soul."

As Jeniah pondered his meaning, the teacher pursed his lips and whistled. Gerheart called in return and then swooped down, landing on Skonas's gloved arm. Skonas nodded to the princess and turned to the door.

"Where are you going?" Jeniah asked.

"We're done for today." Skonas exited without another word.

Chapter Four

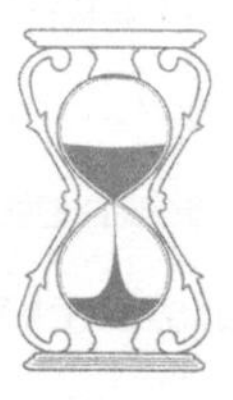

No one living in Emberfell could remember the last time a gloamingtide fête followed Tower Rise so closely. A quick look through the history books found no such instance in the last two hundred years.

But death never claimed monarchs on a convenient schedule. It was impossible to predict whether the two events—one a calendar mainstay, the other a jape of fate—might coincide. Now, they did. Just three short days following the Monarchy's tribute to the Queen Ascendant, preparations began across the land for the welcoming of autumn.

And the arrival of the Crimson Hoods.

Word came the day after Tower Rise that Emberfell would receive the Crimson Hoods. As mysterious as they were vaunted, the cloaked and silent envoys of the queen visited only one town during each gloamingtide celebration. Their presence was considered a great honor in itself. But no honor was greater than to be *selected* by the Hoods.

Four times a year—one for each gloamingtide that marked the passing of the seasons—the Crimson Hoods took one of the chosen town's residents away to serve the queen. These selected few went to live, so it was said, in one of the Nine Towers. They were lavished, so it was said, with privileges and extravagances previously reserved for the monarch and the monarch's family. In exchange, they performed duties vital to the continued prosperity of all in the land. So it was said.

What these duties were, no one knew. And no one cared. It was a chance to serve the monarch in a way very, very few could. That service was superior to any excess the queen could provide.

Although gloamingtide heralded its official arrival, autumn had been in evidence for some time. An early frost—welcome respite from a particularly warm summer—prompted everyone to don woolly sweaters and caps. The smell of burning leaves and cooking spices promised evenings of comforting fires and even more comforting food.

Aon stood atop a ladder, cheerfully removing the bright banners from Tower Rise that hung from the rooftop thatching. Below, her father sat using a nail as a needle and thin rope as thread to pierce through colorful leaves and small gourds, making garlands that would replace the banners. When he finished a strand, he wove a glossy purple ribbon throughout. The ribbon had been Aon's idea.

While Aon hid a sorrow no one in Emberfell would understand, it was not her permanent state. Most days, Aon was *very* happy. Today, for example. She loved autumn, and the gloamingtide festivals were among her most cherished memories. She looked forward to drinking spiced cider later that night until she got sick, after the Crimson Hoods had taken one of Emberfell's lucky citizens with them to Nine Towers. Aon was not incapable of happiness. But she enjoyed her secret bouts of grief like a wicked indulgence.

Aon moved the ladder across the street, and her father fed strands of garland up to her.

"I forgot to tell you," her father said, grinning. "Jackdaw Fen will be gracing all with a new song at the celebration tonight."

Aon giggled. Her father belonged to a trio of bards. They called themselves Jackdaw Fen. Every gloamingtide, they entertained the whole town with songs around the bonfire. "What's this one about?" she asked.

"Wrote it myself," her father said proudly. "It's based on the legend of Pirep and Tali."

Aon applauded. The fable of Pirep and Tali—two girls who got lost in Dreadwillow Carse—had always been one of her favorite bedtime stories. She suspected she liked it because her mother's family tree showed she had ancestors named Pirep and Tali. Her mother had often teased, saying Aon's distant relatives were the same girls from the tale. But it was just make-believe.

Aon also liked the story because it was sad. The girls got lost in the Carse and never came out. But, of course, the people of Emberfell still thought it had a happy ending. Because nothing made them sad or scared or heartbroken. Nothing.

Aon raised her arms, very much resembling the statue of Queen Sula. "I look forward to a command performance," she said in her most regal voice.

Aon and her father laughed as Aon carefully tied the first garland to the chimney of their neighbor, Mrs. Grandwyn. It stretched across the road to the awning of their house. The sunlight caught the purple ribbon, making the garland shimmer.

"It's beautiful!" her father declared. "You've outdone yourself this year, rose blossom."

Aon looked sharply down at her father, whose eyes immediately darted the other way. Rose blossom. The nickname her mother had given Aon. He hadn't used it for three years. It was the smallest of slips, yet it told Aon so much. Somewhere deep under his ever-present smile, in some place his mind reserved for the oldest of dreams, her father still remembered.

Now, as he busied himself with the next garland, Aon's heart ached to pose the questions that had gone unanswered for years.

Do you miss Mother?

How often do you think of her?

If you could speak to her one more time, what would you say?

Aon had her own answers to these questions, so many answers that all she wanted to do was say them out loud to someone who could help her understand them. But it would never happen. It would mean talking about her mother. And no one, anywhere, did that. Ever.

There were times—like this—when Aon wondered

if everyone's happiness was really a mask. Was it possible the other people of the land could feel all the emotions she felt—the grief, the anger—and hid them in the name of pleasing their monarch?

But these slips—when people were on the verge of remembering someone's absence or expressing a feeling other than joy—only ever lasted a moment, until the twinkle in their eyes returned, vanquishing unpleasant thoughts.

No. Aon was the only one who felt this way. She was the only one who was broken.

"Come on," Aon's father boomed merrily. "We've got twelve more to hang before the Crimson Hoods arrive."

Aon did as she was told. And she smiled.

The sun was but a sliver disappearing behind the mountains when the Crimson Hoods arrived.

A watchman in a turret at the western edge of town spotted the pair coming and rang the bell. Everyone everywhere dropped what they were doing and spilled out into the streets. Aon and her father had been finishing their dinner when they heard the bell. They fussed with each other's clothes—he straightened her dress; she smoothed his wrinkly shirt—before heading out into the street.

The townsfolk lined up in front of their houses and stood up tall. There was no guarantee that the Hoods would visit your street, but you wanted to be ready if they did. Aon slipped her hand into her father's. She almost gasped as she saw the two Hoods round the corner and make their way slowly down her own street. Someone *she knew* was being chosen.

The Hoods walked closer and closer. The queen's envoys wore the long robes of monks, with voluminous cowls stained a deep, dark red, the exact color of a sunset heralding an oncoming storm. Their faces were never, ever seen. They slowed as they approached Aon's house.

For a moment, Aon thought they were going to choose *her*. It was rare, but not unheard of, for the Hoods to select a child. Her heart and mind raced; her heart marveled at the thrill of serving the queen, and her mind filled with questions she would ask.

Why choose me, Your Majesty? Did I please you in some way? What is Dreadwillow Carse? Why does it make me feel sad? Why do you want us to be happy so badly?

Am I really broken?

Yes. That was the first question she needed answered.

The Hoods stopped in front of Aon's father.

Each Hood reached out an arm and laid it gently on her father's shoulders.

Aon's throat burned with bile, even as her father's face beamed with pride. A cheer rang up and down the streets of Emberfell. Aon couldn't move. She hardly noticed when her father bent over and pulled her in tightly.

"Can you believe it?" he whispered. She could feel his tears of joy as he pressed his cheek to hers.

No. He was happy? He was being taken away from his daughter. How could he be happy? She had no one left. *What about me?* Aon thought.

"You will be cared for," her father assured her. "And I will always love you."

"Will I see you again?" It was the only thing she could think to ask.

Father held her chin up so their eyes met. "Aon, the greatest thing that can happen to us is here now. You *will* be happy, I promise."

He hadn't answered her question.

Aon tied her last strand of purple ribbon to her father's crutch. She needed to know he'd have *one* reminder of her. Then she kissed him on the cheek as the Hoods led him away.

The revelry grew louder as Aon's father passed their neighbors, limping and waving. Aon barely noticed when Mrs. Grandwyn took her hand and led her to the house across the street. She had seen this happen before. If the Crimson Hoods claimed a family's provider, a neighbor would take in the rest of the family. No questions were asked. No tears were shed. Emberfell took care of its own.

Aon felt it immediately. Once the Hoods turned the corner, once her father was out of sight, everything returned to normal on their street. No more words were spoken about Aon's father. Later tonight, at the bonfire, it would be as if he had never been there. Jackdaw Fen would perform, now as a duo. From here on out, Aon Greenlaw would always have been a member of the Grandwyn family. The wound left behind by Aon's father's exit would be closed just that quickly.

And life—the life they all knew and loved and embraced and never questioned—would go on.

Chapter Five

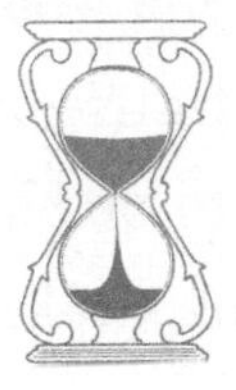

After four days with Skonas, Jeniah had arrived at a conclusion: Her first duty as queen would be passing a law with severe penalties for anyone who answered a question with another question.

That was all her new teacher seemed able to do. When she asked him how best to settle a dispute between land owners, he would ask, "Why do you suppose land owners argue?" When she asked the proper way to host dignitaries from across the Monarchy, he would ask, "Are you sure there's just one proper way?" This went on from sunrise to sundown. He'd imparted no lessons since that first one: *You are your own best teacher.*

Jeniah went to bed each night, furious that she wasn't any closer to learning how to be queen than before Skonas had arrived. She didn't *know* how to be her own best teacher. She would stare at the canopy over her bed, trying to figure out why her mother had selected this odd man to be her tutor. While she believed Skonas to be a fool, she knew her mother wasn't, not by any means.

Three times a day, Jeniah joined the queen at her bedside for meals. Her mother would ask, "How are your lessons with Skonas?" And Jeniah would report, "Fine." She was reluctant to admit that she didn't understand what her tutor was doing. Nor would she admit that she didn't know why the queen had chosen him. Queens—even future queens—she reasoned, should know these things. So Jeniah hid her ignorance and prayed she'd figure it out.

Every day, she would meet Skonas in the library after breakfast. They would stare at each other silently across the table. She waited for him to give her an order, set her a lesson. Most often, he took out a pair of knitting needles and began to craft what Jeniah could only guess was a sock for his lengthy beard.

When she could take it no longer, she'd collect some books and continue searching for information about the Carse. All the while, Skonas simply sat there—knitting and humming a peculiar tune he'd been humming for hours on end, day after day—until Jeniah asked a question about something she'd read.

And then he would answer with a question.

On the fifth day, Jeniah stopped going to the library. She didn't see the point. When Sirilla, the lady's maid who helped the princess dress each morning, came to her chambers, Jeniah flatly refused to get out of bed. "Why should I bother?" she asked. "I'm not learning anything. He's not teaching me what I need to know."

"Begging your pardon, Your Highness," Sirilla said, "but you *are* the Queen Ascendant. He cannot refuse your command."

Jeniah considered this. Never once had she used her authority to get what she wanted. *Kind words win hearts; cross words turn them*, her mother had always said. And it was advice that had worked for them both. Until now.

Unhappy that it had come to this, Jeniah quickly dressed and went in search of her tutor. He *would* answer her questions today. But she found the library empty. Asking around the castle, Jeniah learned he was in the gardens just outside Lithe Tower.

Jeniah found Skonas standing near a six-foot-tall stone obelisk with a great flame on top that burned morning, noon, and night. This was a memorial to all past monarchs. An inscription ran along the monolith's base: *In the name of peace*. Skonas stood with his head bowed, as if praying.

Jeniah summoned her best royal voice. It was the tone her mother used to let people know she would not be swayed from her course. She walked right up to Skonas, hands planted firmly on her hips, and leveled her most serious stare at him. "I have questions for you."

Skonas raised his head. "Questions are the lamplight that lead us from the darkness. And you know what lamplight really is, yes?" He leaned in and met her serious stare. "*Fire*. You should tread carefully, Your Highness."

But Jeniah wouldn't be intimidated. "Then surely answers extinguish the flames."

"So you're saying answers return you to the dark?"

"Well, n-no . . . I—I mean . . ."

"How can you seek answers if you don't know what they really are?"

Jeniah growled. He was being tricky again.

"As Queen Ascendant, I command you to answer me: Why can't I go into Dreadwillow Carse?"

The tutor sniffed and turned his gaze to the sky. He held out his forearm, wrapped in his falconer's glove. "Why do you think?"

The princess stifled a volcanic scream.

But she continued with her firm, royal voice. "I've been told that if any monarch goes into Dreadwillow Carse, the Monarchy will fall. If I'm to be queen, I need to know what that means. Is it a prophecy?"

Skonas tilted his head thoughtfully. Then he said, "I don't believe in prophecies. They're too . . . absolute. People are too fickle to adhere to absolutes. Prophecies are stories that cheat so the storyteller can pretend he knew all along what would happen.

"What you've been told is a *warning*. Quite different. You've heard plenty of those in your life, I'd imagine. 'If you touch the fire, then you'll get burned.' 'If you play in the rain, then you'll catch a cold.' If. Then. It's a choice. Prophecies don't offer a choice. But warnings do. And living is all about choices, wouldn't you agree?"

This was the most Skonas had said to Jeniah since that first day. It seemed using her authority as

Queen Ascendant was the key. She continued. "But those warnings make sense," she said. "At some point, someone touched a fire and got burned. So they warned others. No monarch has ever entered the Carse, or the Monarchy would have fallen by now. How can you warn someone about something that clearly has never happened?"

A smile bullied its way onto Skonas's lips. "Strangely clever," he said. Skonas said that to Jeniah a lot. He seemed to think it was a compliment. But Jeniah could never be sure.

Overhead, Gerheart cried. A moment later, the falcon landed on Skonas's arm. The tutor fed his bird a chunk of bread and then said, "Not all warnings are perfect, you know." He held his gloved hand over the fire atop the obelisk. "You see? I'm not getting burned."

Jeniah rolled her eyes. "Of course not. You're wearing a glove."

"But the warning doesn't say, 'If you touch the fire, you'll get burned . . . unless you're wearing a glove.' Even warnings need to be heeded with caution."

"So, you're saying there are ways around certain warnings?"

"I'm saying," Skonas said, sending Gerheart flying

with a flick of his wrist, "that all warnings must be considered."

Jeniah reeled at the idea. Not the idea that warnings should be considered, but that Skonas was actually making sense. "Where did the warning come from?" she asked.

"Where does any ancient knowledge come from? It's handed down through the generations until the significance of the person who first said it is lost to the winds of time. Sometimes, we lose their name altogether. And despite this, the knowledge gets repeated and repeated over and over."

Jeniah's nose wrinkled. She didn't like not knowing who had issued the warning in the first place. It could have been anyone. Following a rule *just because* it had always been followed felt strange. She liked to understand rules. She needed to.

"And you know what's interesting?" Skonas said. "The same is true of lies. Say a lie over and over, and people will start to think it's true."

Which was *exactly* what Jeniah had been thinking. Suppose the warning had been spread by someone who had stolen something from the royal family. Perhaps they'd hidden it in the Carse, and to keep the family from investigating, spread a rumor that entering the Carse would mean disaster. The idea was far-fetched, of course . . . but still possible.

On the other hand, Jeniah had first heard the warning from the queen. Jeniah trusted her mother, and her mother believed in the warning with all her heart. Maybe the queen knew more than Skonas. Maybe she had a very good reason to believe the Monarchy would fall if a monarch entered the Carse.

But maybe only one held any value: Maybe the warning was wrong.

"One other thing," Skonas said. He leaned over until their faces were a mere hairbreadth apart. For days, the tutor had been amiable. Jovial, even. The look on his face as he peered into Jeniah's eyes made him appear more serious than she'd ever seen him. "If you think you'll get anywhere with me by throwing royal commands around, you are gravely mistaken. I come to teach Ascendants out of courtesy to the reigning monarch. I am not a royal subject, and you have no power over me. Remember that."

Skonas whistled. Gerheart swooped down and perched on the tutor's arm. Skonas nodded to the princess and walked off, leaving her alone at the memorial.

Warnings must be considered, Skonas had said. So

Jeniah considered. She closed her eyes and repeated the centuries-old warning over and over again to herself softly. After an hour of this—an hour filled with fervent whispers and deep thought—the princess came to a realization that sent her running to her bedchambers in search of her longest hooded cloak.

The warning said *she* couldn't enter the Carse.

It didn't say she couldn't send in someone else.

Chapter Six

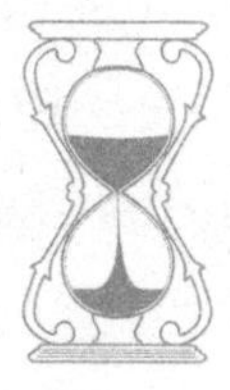

EVERYWHERE SHE WENT, AON SMILED.

She traded jokes with the butcher when she went shopping for Mrs. Grandwyn. She led her classmates in singing the joyous songs that celebrated Emberfell's bountiful harvest at the autumn pageant. And she cheerfully read bedtime stories to Mrs. Grandwyn's youngest children—her new siblings.

Happiness was her only choice now. In the week since her father had been taken by the Crimson Hoods to serve the queen, Aon had come to believe one simple fact: she was being punished for her sadness.

It was the only explanation. Somehow, the queen

had been spying on her from atop one of the royal towers. She had seen Aon enter the Carse and come out crying. The loss of her father was the price of her sorrow.

So Aon swore she'd never return to the Carse. No matter how badly her sorrow festered deep within, no matter how strongly she heard the marsh's plaintive tune in her dreams every night, no matter how sure she remained that the Carse could fix what was broken in her—she knew she could never go back. And maybe if she behaved the way the queen wanted and lived her life in complete happiness, she would get to see her father again.

But then she'd remember the look on her father's face when the Hoods had chosen him. He was ecstatic. He was honored. He wasn't the least bit sad he was leaving his daughter behind. Aon shouldn't have been surprised. He'd never once admitted to missing his wife. Why would he feel differently about his daughter?

Knowing she could never win, Aon melted into the Grandwyn family. She fought off the sadness that still tugged at her heart. She *would* be happy, as she was supposed to be.

One day, Aon was in the barn behind her parents'

house, stoking the hot coals in her mother's forge. *Aon's* forge, now. *Aon's* house, when she came of age. But something told her she would always think of the forge as her mother's and the house as her parents'. The memories were too great.

It was here, near the heat of the fire they shared, that her mother had made the most wonderful glass creations. Vases, sculptures, pots—there wasn't much Aon's mother couldn't craft. She'd even made the statue of Queen Sula near the mayor's house. From an early age, Aon had studied glassblowing at her mother's side. This place was Aon's last connection to her.

Nearby, Laius, Mrs. Grandwyn's long-necked son, gripped a tall metal rod and gleefully sang Jackdaw Fen's ballad of Pirep and Tali. Aon giggled. Even during her saddest moments, she'd always found the boy's mirth contagious. The pair had grown up just across the street from each other. There was much she liked about Laius. He was sweet, if frequently befuddled and easily distracted. He was curious, a trait they shared. And that singing voice—clear and melodious—had always been his greatest skill.

Which was precisely why Aon and Laius were at the forge. For all his good traits, Laius had yet to prove adept at anything besides singing. Few believed the boy could use his voice—glorious as it was—as a trade. So, months before the arrival of the Crimson Hoods, Laius's and Aon's fathers had agreed that Aon would teach Laius glassblowing. She'd watched them shake hands, sealing the deal. And she'd smiled, even though she knew there would be difficult days ahead.

Most of Aon's time was spent making sure her easily distracted new brother didn't burn himself. Today was no exception. As he swayed roughly from side to side, singing the final verse of his song, Aon gently guided him farther from the forge's radiant, scalding heart.

Once he'd finished singing, she moved him closer. "Take your time," Aon said. She stirred the pool of white-hot sand with a steel paddle, watching the sand melt into liquid glass. Laius dipped the metal rod he held into the molten pool. He turned the rod slowly, gathering thick strands of glowing fluid. When he had enough—the glass was as large as a beehive—he pulled the rod out and held it up.

"Very good," Aon said. "And next?"

Laius pressed the cool end of the rod to his mouth and blew gently. The red molten glass on the other end expanded into a bulb. He pressed the bulb against the edge of a marble table, collapsing the middle slightly.

He continued to press and blow until he had two bulbs joined by a narrow shaft.

"The hourglass must be perfectly shaped," Aon reminded him. "Otherwise, the sands won't flow smoothly."

Laius nodded and, as he did, his chin knocked against the rod. Jarred, the shaft that joined the two bulbs broke, and both fell with a hiss into a bucket of water below. The boy laughed at his failure, the closest he would ever come to disappointment.

"Your next hourglass will be perfect," Aon said, patting his shoulder. But he needed no encouragement. A smile on his face, Laius reached for a fresh rod and dipped it into the liquid glass.

"Now this time," Aon said, "I want you to turn the rod while you're forming the shaft. That way, you can—"

"Why do you go into the Carse?"

In her dreams, Aon had heard her father ask that very question. In her dreams, she fumbled for an excuse, all the while avoiding Father's fierce and unrelenting gaze. Thankfully, the question had always disappeared when she woke. It was no small surprise that, when the question finally came for real, it was from Laius.

"I've seen you," he said. "You don't do it often. I've followed you to the edge of town, but I can never get that close. It's a strange place, the Carse."

He said this all with a gentle smile on his face, gathering fresh molten glass for another go at the hourglass. He wasn't accusing her. He hadn't caught her. He was just curious.

"I don't do that," she said, and then added, "Anymore."

"But you used to. Why?"

Aon considered telling the truth. For three years, all she'd wanted was to discuss her feelings with someone. But looking into her adopted brother's bright, blank eyes, she knew it wouldn't be enough. She didn't need someone to talk to. She needed someone to understand. And sweet, awkward Laius never would. Never could.

"I'm not what anyone thinks I am, Laius," she said. It was the closest, she thought, she might ever come to a confession. When the boy's face told her he didn't quite comprehend, she said simply, "It makes me happy."

Which, of course, made no sense. Anyone who'd ever gotten too close to the bog's edge knew it was not a place where anyone could be happy. But it was the only answer anyone in Emberfell would understand.

Laius tilted his head in his charmingly baffled way and grinned. "The queen wants all her subjects to be happy," he said.

With a final twist of the rod, he held up his masterpiece. The hourglass looked more like a pyramid. The boy's smirk suggested he knew he'd failed again.

Aon squeezed his shoulder. "Your next hourglass will be perfect," she reminded him.

"You said that about this one," he said.

"But you didn't make an hourglass," she replied. "Your next *hourglass* will be perfect." She pointed at the fire. "Now, try again."

And like that, Laius plunged the rod into the forge, fishing for liquid glass with renewed vigor. He sang out in a voice sure and clear. Aon smiled to herself. If she could no longer use the mysterious singing in the Carse to ease her sorrow, her new brother's voice would do almost as nicely.

IT WAS WELL after dark when Aon pushed Mrs. Grandwyn's wheelbarrow to the edge of town. She emptied a mound of old vegetables onto a compost heap. She was turning to go home, when she heard a cry in the dark.

"Help!"

The voice was faint but piercing. Aon looked

around but saw no one. Then the cry came again, from the west. Beyond Emberfell's borders.

Near the Carse.

With lantern in hand, Aon ran toward the pleas and immediately felt the Carse's dark embrace. Foreboding and dread prickled at her flesh. For just a moment, she welcomed that sensation. She'd missed it.

Rounding a bend, she spotted a girl on the ground. Shrouded in a long cloak, the girl was wrestling great leafy vines as they snaked out from the Carse and wrapped themselves around her body.

"Stay still!" Aon called out as she ran to the girl's side.

"It's . . . crushing . . . me . . . ," the stranger gasped from under a hood that hid her face.

"The vines are attracted to movement," Aon said as she knelt at the girl's side. "Just relax. Here, take my hand. I won't let you go, but you have to stop squirming."

With a whimper, the girl did as she was told. The pair remained absolutely still. Almost immediately, the vines stopped crawling. A moment later, the vines released their grip and slunk back into the darkness of the Carse.

Once the danger was over, Aon helped the girl to her feet. "We should move away. Are you hurt?"

She led the girl back toward Emberfell. The stranger brushed off her cloak. "I'm . . . I'm okay. Just shaken."

"You should be more careful," Aon said, laughing as she scolded. "Everyone knows to stay away from the mirebramble."

The girl seemed confused and then laughed herself. "You're right. I should probably know better. But I've never seen it before."

Aon smiled. "Then you can't be from Emberfell. Where are you from?"

"Not far," the girl said, pulling back her hood.

Aon immediately knew her face. She'd seen the girl just a year earlier in a royal parade that had wended its way through Emberfell as part of a tour of the Monarchy. Aon had never seen anyone else quite like the girl. The beautiful dark skin, the silky black hair.

It was Jeniah, the Queen Ascendant.

Chapter Seven

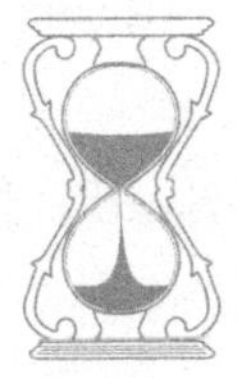

"THANK YOU."

Jeniah drank greedily from the mug Aon offered. The spiced cider warmed her insides, replacing the chill that had settled in her bones since her trek from Nine Towers. To venture out to Emberfell, she'd chosen the cloak that would best hide her identity. Sadly, it wasn't the cloak best suited to fending off the cool autumn evening.

The house Aon had brought her to was dark, except for two small candles the girl had lit. Aon had known where to go to find the matches, as if she knew the house well. But, clearly, no one lived here. It was too quiet. And though it was filled with furniture, Jeniah couldn't help feeling the house seemed empty.

Jeniah peered through the dim light at Aon, who sat hugging her knees to her chest. Aon couldn't take her eyes off the princess.

"It's very dark," Jeniah said. "Can we light more candles?"

The girl shook her head. "It would attract attention. And you said you wanted to keep your visit a secret."

Jeniah felt her cheeks flush. So much for exploring the town unnoticed. She hadn't even set foot in Emberfell before her presence had been revealed. Thankfully, Aon had respected Jeniah's pleas for secrecy and had helped spirit the princess through the shadows of the town.

"Whose house is this?" Jeniah asked.

Aon opened her mouth but then closed it, as if she'd suddenly thought better of what she was going to say. When she finally spoke, she said, "How are you feeling? Getting too close to the Carse can be . . . dangerous."

"I'm fine," Jeniah said. "The bramble didn't hurt me. A few scratches, that's all."

Aon leaned in. "But . . . how do you *feel*?"

Jeniah wasn't sure she understood the question. "I'm fine. I told you." But she could tell by the look in Aon's eyes that it was the wrong answer. "How *should* I feel?"

Aon took a cinnamon stick and stirred her own mug of cider. "Most people who go near the Carse . . . There's something about it. People feel the urge to get away."

"Well, I'm not surprised," Jeniah said. "The mirebramble is very dangerous."

But Aon shook her head. "It's not just that. Their skin starts to crawl. And they don't know quite why, but everything in their brains and in their hearts tells them they don't want to be anywhere near."

"You mean they feel scared?"

"No. Not exactly. They usually move away before they can feel truly scared." Aon eyed the princess curiously. "But not you?"

Jeniah returned the girl's inquiring stare. The princess had indeed felt scared when the mirebramble snagged her ankles and pulled her down. But that was to be expected. Aside from that . . .

"No," the princess admitted.

"It's because you're part of the royal family. At least, I think so."

Jeniah wasn't sure what to make of this. She'd always been told that the people of the Monarchy were happy all the time and that it would be her job as monarch to make sure they stayed that way. Royal decree was keeping her from entering the Carse. Maybe *something else* kept the rest of the world out. If so, how would she find someone to explore on her behalf?

"You talk about it as if . . . well, as if the Carse has some sort of *power* over people." Jeniah spoke calmly, but her heart thundered with hope. Was she right? Was there magic in the Carse?

"You could say that," Aon said. "There's a reason everyone avoids it."

"You didn't," Jeniah said. "You didn't even hesitate to help me."

The girl looked away, almost as if she were ashamed. Then she said, "I . . . I was so sorry to hear about the queen. She's always been good and kind."

Jeniah studied Aon carefully. She couldn't remember anyone—anyone who wasn't royalty—ever offering her condolences before. Jeniah was beginning to suspect that, even if the Carse was able to drive people away, this girl wasn't so easily influenced.

"Thank you," Jeniah said. "If the Carse is so strange, I was fortunate you came along."

"How long will you be in Emberfell, Your Highness?" Aon asked.

Jeniah's lips pulled back. Her plan involved coming to Emberfell to seek someone who would enter the Carse and report back to her. But that was all she had. She found herself wishing now that she'd spent more time considering *how* to do that.

"You seem to know a lot about Dreadwillow Carse," the princess said.

Aon shrugged. "Everyone around here knows about the mirebramble."

"Do you know what's inside the Carse?"

The girl stared into the flames. "Is it . . . Is it illegal to go in there?"

Jeniah shook her head, puzzled. This brave girl who'd rescued her only a short while ago suddenly seemed almost . . . scared. But that wasn't possible. Was it? "No, not at all," Jeniah answered. "You see . . . I came to Emberfell to find out what's in the Carse. Can I trust you, Aon?"

The girl nodded. Jeniah folded her hands and told the story of the ancient warning and the dire consequences that would follow if she entered the Carse. She explained how she didn't feel she could be a proper queen until she understood what was so dangerous about it.

Aon listened closely. When the princess was done speaking, she said, "The warning says no *monarch* can enter the Carse. But you're not the monarch yet. You could enter if you wanted."

Jeniah held up the opal ring on her finger. "Once I became Queen Ascendant, I became the monarch by royal law. My coronation after my mother's death will be a formality, the event that confers on me the title 'majesty.' So I'm here to find someone else who will explore the Carse for me and learn its secrets. I need someone who—"

"I'll go." Aon hadn't even hesitated.

The princess smiled. "I appreciate your eagerness, but I think someone older—"

"You won't find anyone else," Aon said. Then she swallowed hard. "Forgive me for interrupting, but no one else will go near the Carse. I've told you. It has ways of keeping people out."

Jeniah studied the girl, whose eyes had filled with something familiar. *Hunger*, Jeniah thought. "But then how could *you* go?"

Aon said flatly, "Because I've been in there before."

So the girl *did* know about the Carse.

"What have you seen?" Jeniah said quickly. "Is it dangerous?" *Is it magical?*

Aon gnawed on her lower lip. "Well . . . There's the bog, of course. Dreadwillow trees, lots of them. And . . ." The girl paused. Then she said, "And I've heard singing."

"Singing?" Did someone *live* in the Carse?

"I don't know where it comes from," Aon admitted. "It might just be the wind in the trees. But I've always wanted to find out. I'm sure if I were to just go in deeper, I'd know more. And I could see what else is there."

Jeniah could hardly contain her excitement. Suddenly, the idea of learning what was in the Carse was very real. This could actually work. It was almost too easy.

And as quickly as she'd gotten her hopes up, they crashed down around her. Yes. *Too* easy. The more real the possibility of success became, the more Jeniah's plan seemed foolish. How could she ask a girl her own age to do something so dangerous? The mirebramble alone suggested that Dreadwillow Carse was more perilous than she'd first imagined, possibly even deadly. "I appreciate your offer, but I didn't think this through. I'm sorry. I must return to Nine Towers. Please don't tell anyone I was here." She started to leave.

"You need my help, Princess," Aon said, her voice insistent but also pleading. "You won't find anyone else who can, I promise you. And if I don't help, you'll never know what's in the Carse. I can do this."

Jeniah wished she had just taken the cider, thanked the girl for her help, and gone off in search of someone else. But Aon had ignited something in the princess. *Singing*. The girl had heard singing. Jeniah *had* to know where it came from. And if she looked for an adult, there was every chance whoever she found would report back to Nine Towers and tell the queen what Jeniah was doing. She couldn't have that. Aon, at least, seemed trustworthy. And if the girl's knowledge of the mirebramble was any indication, she surely was clever enough to avoid the Carse's other dangers.

The princess removed the clasp on her cloak—a jeweled medallion with bronze and chrome framework shaped like a falcon in flight—and handed it to Aon. "The royal crest. If anyone questions you, show them this. It says that you are my emissary and act on behalf of the Monarchy. This will give you entry anywhere."

Aon held the crest tight to her heart. "I'll need some time to prepare," she said. "Two days, then I'll go. I'll send letters to the castle and tell you what I find."

"When I have all the information I need," Jeniah said, "I'll issue a royal proclamation, praising your loyalty and bravery. Your name will be celebrated—"

"I don't want praise," Aon interrupted. "Or money or glory. If I do this for you, you must do something for me."

Jeniah blinked. No one had ever demanded anything from her before. "And what's that?"

The girl regarded her, stone-faced. "Return my father to me."

Jeniah suppressed a smile. So *that* was why the girl had been so keen to help. Aon didn't want just any reward. There was something she needed in return.

Intrigued, the princess said, "Tell me more."

THE TWO GIRLS spoke for hours, weaving a web of promises and whispers. In no time, they were exchanging stories of their lives and laughing like the oldest of friends. The princess saw a kindred spirit—daring and inquisitive—with the ability to do and feel things no commoner should be able. And Aon saw a girl who would soon be alone in the world. With every hour that passed, another link was added to the bond between them. They could feel it.

Before they parted ways, each swore to help the other.

And each told the other a lie.

Chapter Eight

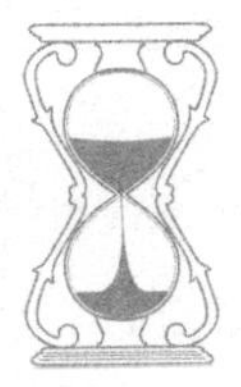

The Monarchy had few laws. In a land of plenty, where kindness prevailed and deceit was mere fantasy, hardly any regulations were needed. Even Dreadwillow Carse, with its mirebramble and other assorted dangers, wasn't formally forbidden. And though Aon was no expert on the rules that governed the land, she was fairly certain one of the laws must be "Do not lie to royalty."

But that was what Aon had done. More or less.

In boasting that she'd already been in the Carse, Aon had omitted one key fact. She had never gone more than thirty-two steps into the marsh's bleak interior. She had never passed the hook-shaped rock. She couldn't. She'd tried. Oh, how she'd tried. Time after time, she'd failed to find what she sought. And yet she continued. The Carse held answers for her. She knew that.

And, it seemed, the Carse held answers for Princess Jeniah as well.

But Aon's past efforts were meaningless now. She possessed the royal crest, the symbol of ultimate authority. And because the princess had proven immune to the Carse's power, surely the crest would get Aon deep into the Carse at last.

That was, if she wasn't arrested. If lying to royalty wasn't against the law, certainly making demands of a royal must be. In the moment, Aon hadn't given it a second thought. The words had tumbled from her mouth without regard to possible consequences. This was how badly she wanted her father back. The threat of danger had held little fear. Now she felt a deep and all-consuming guilt at having lied to her sovereign. And an absolute terror that the princess might seek revenge.

For all Aon knew, Jeniah would return shortly with a battalion of soldiers who would arrest Aon for her boldness. She would be the first person to be thrown into prison in hundreds of years. All because she was broken. All because she couldn't control her sadness.

Aon waited to be arrested. But no one came for her. The princess had left Emberfell, promising to uphold her end of the bargain. Which meant Aon would have to honor hers. And when it became clear she was not in trouble for insisting that Princess Jeniah return Aon's father, she set to work.

As the sun went down, Aon took a spade from her parents' barn and then crept to the east end of town, far from the Carse. She entered the woods where two oak trees bowed in the middle, forming an arch. From the arch, she counted fifty steps dead ahead. At the stream that interrupted her path, she turned north and counted another fifty steps. She paused only to glance quickly over her shoulder. A shadow, following in her footsteps, darted behind a tree.

She continued on, her fiftieth step bringing her to three saplings that formed a triangle. Lighting a lantern against the encroaching night, she then stood in the center of the triangle and started digging. When the spade stopped with a *thunk*, she knelt and pawed at the soft earth with her hands. She brushed the dirt away to reveal a rectangular wooden box. Opening the lid, Aon removed an hourglass as long as her forearm.

Set in a silver frame, the hourglass's bulbs were perfectly shaped and completely flawless. Golden flakes—more like glitter than sand—filled the bottom bulb. On the side of the hourglass, as if etched with early-morning frost, was a set of wavy lines that curved around one another. Up close, they looked like nothing more than lines. But, on taking a step back, she saw clearly this was a rose in bloom—Aon's mother's trademark. Despite having just been in the cold ground, the hourglass felt warm in Aon's hand.

It felt like it belonged there. It made her hand feel whole again.

"What are you doing?"

Aon pretended to jump at the question. She turned. Laius peered curiously at her from the shadows.

"You followed me," she said.

She did her best to sound surprised. But she'd known all along he was there. Laius had made little effort to hide. Of course, Aon had made no effort to throw him off her trail. She'd led him here on purpose, but he could never know that.

The boy nodded and knelt next to Aon. He couldn't take his eyes off the hourglass. Aon handed the timekeeper to him. Laius ran his palm against the smooth glass, marveling all the while. Aon couldn't help but smile. This was what he'd been working with her to achieve. She knew he'd never seen one so perfect before.

"It's beautiful," Laius said. "Why is it buried in the woods?"

Aon studied his face. She had known Laius all her life. His hands, big for a boy his age, were clumsy. But what he lacked in grace, he made up in loyalty. Aon needed someone loyal. She knew she couldn't perform the princess's task alone. The trick would be getting Laius to help without betraying Jeniah's trust.

"I was thinking," Aon said, "that maybe you're having trouble blowing an hourglass because you don't have one to look at for an example. Maybe the next time we're in the forge, you could look at this one."

Laius's eyes lit up, as if Aon had handed him the final piece of a puzzle he'd been trying to solve for ages. "But why did you bury it?"

Aon considered lying, but her late-night talk with the princess had made her bolder. "Laius," she said, "do you remember my mother?"

The boy smiled, but his brow furrowed in confusion. She could see that he *did* remember Mother. But, just like everyone else, the overwhelming happiness rendered such memories meaningless. It was as if he knew what she meant if she said "cup" or "towel" but couldn't summon the words to describe them.

"She taught me how to blow glass," Aon continued. "She made this herself. It was the first time she'd ever gotten an hourglass right. She loved it more than any other glass she blew. She always told me she'd give it to me once I turned eighteen."

Aon wasn't even sure Laius was listening. His eyes had become glassy, his gaze unfixed. It was the look anyone in Emberfell gave when Aon talked about her mother. Or when they got too close to the Carse.

But where any adult with that look on his face would have excused himself and walked away by now, Laius remained in the hourglass's thrall. Which meant Aon had a chance.

At times, being the only person in all the land capable of trickery came in handy.

"Once my mother was gone," Aon pressed on, "I don't think my father wanted to remember her. I woke up one day, and it was as if she'd never been there. He'd removed everything that ever belonged to her from the house."

She pressed her fingers against the glass and swallowed. "Except this. I had borrowed it from Mother. It was under my bed when Father collected her belongings. He didn't know I had it. And I couldn't risk him taking it as well, so I hid it here."

Aon watched Laius carefully. His dim expression fluttered between a smile and a look of total bewilderment. How would he react to all this? Would he tell Mrs. Grandwyn about the hourglass? Would someone come to take it from her, deciding her mother was best forgotten by all?

Aon took Laius's hands and helped him turn the hourglass upside down. The golden sand inside the top bulb slowly trickled down to the bottom. The grains twinkled, catching bits of firelight as they fell. Laius gasped. Aon knew what he was feeling. The hourglass's beauty often took her own breath away.

"She loved making hourglasses, my mother," Aon said. "She said, 'You always know where you stand with them.' She thought they were the only truly fair things in the world."

"Why?"

"We all come from different backgrounds. Farmers, millers, blacksmiths, tailors . . . But we all get the same amount of time each day to do with as we please. See here?" She pointed to the falling sand. "I've just given us each an hour. There's so much we could do before the last grain tumbles down. It all depends on the choices we make."

Aon's eyes flitted across the boy's face, searching for signs of understanding.

"We should go back to town," Laius said, reaching for her hand.

"My mother used to go into the Carse, too," Aon said, desperate to stop him. It worked. The boy froze and looked at his feet. "Something happened to her. Something no one knows about. I need to find out what that was. And I'm sure the answer lies in the Carse. It's why I go there."

There. She'd done it. Telling this truth felt freeing. And she hadn't mentioned she'd been sent under royal order. Jeniah's secret was safe.

"Laius, I need help. *Your* help."

For the first time, Laius met her eyes. He was not the sort of boy people asked for help.

"Maybe my mother can help you," he said softly.

Aon shook her head. "No, it has to be you. You're the only one I trust."

"You do?"

"I trusted you enough to show you my mother's hourglass, didn't I? You know it makes me happy. And you know I couldn't be happy if someone took it away from me."

For a moment, Aon worried she'd gone too far. There were times she forgot that not only was the sadness she felt unique, but often others couldn't even *understand* the idea of not being happy. It was like asking Laius to imagine a color he'd never seen.

But if Laius didn't understand, he didn't show it. "How can I help?"

"Tomorrow evening," Aon said, "after everyone's gone to sleep, I'm going into the Carse. And I need your help, Laius. I want you to come with me."

The boy's jaw dropped. "No! I can't. It's—"

"You don't have to go in," Aon said quickly. "Just wait at the entrance of the Carse. Once I cross the border, give the hourglass a single turn. I don't want to spend any more than an hour in there. If I'm not back by the time the sands run out, you are to get word to Princess Jeniah."

"The princess?"

"Anyone can request an audience with the royal family. It's the law. Just go to the gates and ask for her. You can say I sent you."

Laius nodded obediently. "Tell the princess."

Worms made of doubt wriggled inside Aon. She hadn't betrayed the princess. Not really. Jeniah had insisted that no one else must know about their agreement, and Aon hadn't told Laius about it. But the princess hadn't felt the way the Carse could creep into your heart. Aon felt safer knowing someone other than Jeniah knew where she'd gone. She wished she felt as sure that the princess would be able to help if something went wrong.

Even so, she smiled and patted her brother's shoulder.

"The princess will know what to do."

Chapter Nine

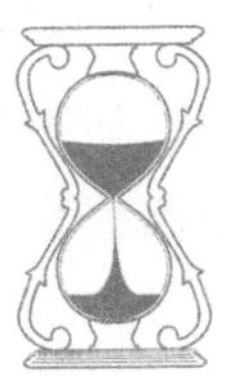

JENIAH KNELT BEFORE THE FIREPLACE IN HER BEDCHAMBERS, watching the flames swirl. She felt defeated. She'd been so proud when she conceived the plan to send someone else into the Carse. It meant she could learn what was there without risking the Monarchy. Surely, these were the sorts of clever ideas that came naturally to queens.

But it was only a small step forward. It was nothing compared to the giant leap backward she'd just been dealt. Even now, with Aon sure to deliver the Carse's secrets, Jeniah watched as a whole new mystery blossomed before her like a dark flower. Sending an emissary to explore the marsh had been an easy solution. Her new problem wouldn't be so quickly solved.

Jeniah had listened carefully as Aon explained how her father had been taken by the Crimson Hoods. Certainly the queen hadn't known she would be orphaning Aon by taking her father into the queen's service to live in a special tower. So maybe the queen could see fit to select someone else and return Aon's father to Emberfell.

Jeniah had assured the girl it could be done. She'd agreed to it as the reward for Aon's help. Aon would send regular reports on what she found in Dreadwillow Carse, and Jeniah would send the girl's father home.

But it was a lie.

Jeniah knew nothing of the tower where special servants of the queen lived.

Jeniah had never before heard of the Crimson Hoods.

At the time, the lie had felt justified. There were many things, Jeniah had reasoned, of which she had not yet been made aware. She'd never been inside her mother's court where they likely discussed such matters. The queen had many agents who performed her bidding throughout the land. Perhaps the existence of the Crimson Hoods would be revealed to Jeniah when Skonas got around to teaching her the other lessons he'd promised.

But . . .

The way Aon had described the Crimson Hoods—mysterious messengers who appeared at the turn of every season—didn't seem right to Jeniah. There was something . . . sinister about it. When Jeniah retired for the evening, she had a new mission: learning about the Crimson Hoods as soon as possible.

The next morning, Jeniah went to her mother's bedchambers to ask what the queen knew about her alleged secret servants. She was greeted outside the door by the Chief Healer. "The queen must not be disturbed, Your Highness," he said gently. "I have given her an elixir to ease the pain that kept her awake during the night. She will sleep for hours." Jeniah tried to insist on waiting at her mother's bedside. But the Chief Healer assured Jeniah that what the queen needed most was solitude.

To distract herself, Jeniah went to her daily appointment with Skonas. When her tutor arrived at the library, humming to his falcon that strange tune he always hummed, she sat across from him and asked, "What can you tell me about the Crimson Hoods?"

Skonas stopped humming and yelped. His eyes widened, whether in shock or fear she couldn't tell. She suspected it was a little of each. The old man lifted his palms to the ceiling and made a circular gesture while muttering under his breath. Startled, Gerheart squawked and retreated to the top of the bookcases.

"What *are* you doing?" the princess asked.

"An ancient ritual," Skonas rasped, "to ward off misfortune. Where did you hear about . . . *them*?"

"I've heard they are secret servants of the monarch," she said. "If I'm to be queen, I should know more about them."

Skonas folded his hands and regarded her closely. "Yes. Yes, I think you're right. It's only fair. As queen, you must know what you're up against."

Jeniah's toes curled in anticipation. This sounded more grave than she'd imagined.

Skonas leaned in and spoke in hushed tones. "Servants of the monarch? Far from it. The Crimson Hoods stalk the silent places of the night, preying on the innocent. They were forged in the shadows cast by the dawn of time. And since the evil beings first walked, they've dedicated themselves to a single purpose: the destruction of the Monarchy."

Jeniah nodded, fighting all the while to hide her

shock. Evil? There had never been, to her knowledge, anything in the Monarchy that could be described as "evil." The word had practically no meaning here. This didn't sound anything like what Aon had reported. And why had Aon believed the Hoods to be the queen's servants?

Unless . . .

Unless the Hoods *posed* as servants of the queen in order to steal away with Her Majesty's most loyal subjects. Unknowingly, Jeniah had stumbled on a conspiracy.

"Again, I must ask," Skonas said. "Where did you hear of them?"

Jeniah was torn. Admitting she'd heard this from Aon meant revealing her plan to learn the secrets of the Carse. But if the Hoods were real and seen recently in Emberfell, then the Monarchy was in danger. She had to act with caution.

"I think I heard Cook mention it," she lied.

Skonas nodded. "Well, she'd know. Most of the staff would know all about the Hoods. They are well versed in ancient knowledge. Wisdom you won't find in books, passed down from generation to generation among the commoners."

Jeniah quietly cursed herself. *Of course* Cook

would know all about this. When she was younger, the princess had spent hours in the kitchen listening to Cook weave tales as she ordered her assistants about. Jeniah wished she'd thought to ask Cook about the Hoods first. The kindly old woman could give Jeniah the information she needed to save the Monarchy *and* rescue Aon's father. And no one would ever need to know about Jeniah's bargain with the brave girl from Emberfell.

The princess thanked her tutor and ran from the library. Until her mother woke, the Monarchy was Jeniah's responsibility. There was a threat to her subjects, and she was going to do something.

She went first to the kitchen to Cook and asked what the kindly matron knew of the Crimson Hoods.

"Very powerful," the old woman said. "They can reach into your chest and turn your very soul to stone."

Next, Jeniah consulted the royal cartographer, Ms. Reynard.

"Before we became a land of bliss, the Crimson Hoods ruled with a savage fist. They say that if the Crimson Hoods ever return, we're all doomed."

Jeniah talked to everyone she could find. All had stories about the horrors of the Crimson Hoods. Each added to her knowledge of this new adversary, but few told her how to fight back. One thing was very clear: the Monarchy was in danger.

It was Mr. Dalcott, the stable keeper, who told her what she most needed to know.

"At the top of Gedric Tower sits the war horn," he said. "It has not been blown for a thousand years, since before the time of the first monarch. It is a cry to battle. When the horn sounds, the wisest scholars gather in the throne room and plan to defend the Monarchy."

The war horn. Of course Jeniah knew of the ancient relic. Her mother had taken her to Gedric Tower and shown it to her a year ago. "One day you will learn," the queen had promised, "how important it is to the Monarchy's heritage." That day, it seemed, had arrived.

As Jeniah ran up the stairs of Gedric Tower, battle plans filled her mind. She would rally the royal troops. She would warn the commoners to avoid the Hoods when they returned. She would expose the evil beasts and protect the Monarchy.

She would be a queen.

Gedric, a tower that twisted upward like a great stone coil, sat on the easternmost part of the Nine Towers' circle of spires. At the very top, Jeniah spotted the great war horn—a crescent of bone and brass that took up nearly the entire room. She puckered her lips, pressed them to the small end of the horn, and blew as hard as she could.

An unearthly shriek echoed throughout the land, glancing off mountains and shooting through trees. Jeniah ran to the throne room, eager to meet with the queen's council to discuss a plan for protecting the Monarchy. But when she got there, she found the scholars huddled in the corner and her mother standing with shaky knees before the throne.

The queen gripped a staff in her weathered hands. It alone kept her standing. As Jeniah approached, Queen Sula placed herself between the princess and the throne.

"Jeniah," the queen whispered, "what is going on?"

The princess reached out. "Mother, the Monarchy is in danger. The ancient evil—the Crimson Hoods—have returned. They're stealing the people of Emberfell. But I've blown the war horn, and I'm preparing to hold council—"

The queen opened her mouth to interrupt but doubled at the waist, seized by a coughing fit. Jeniah gently helped her mother to her knees until the queen recovered.

"Jeniah," Queen Sula said, "the Crimson Hoods are a myth. A fairy tale. They don't exist."

The princess felt a lump in her throat. "No. No, Mother, you see, I know they've been taking people. They're pretending to act in your name. But I have a plan—"

The queen shook her head. "The people of our land dress as the Crimson Hoods as part of a gloamingtide fête. They're symbolic and nothing more. There is no danger. Now, please stop."

Jeniah looked past her mother at the assembled scholars. They whispered to one another, looking perplexed. The queen summoned her strength and dismissed her council with a single gesture. Red-faced, Jeniah helped her mother back to bed; then she stormed to the kitchen.

"You lied to me!" she spat at Cook and the others.

The servants smiled kindly with looks of genuine confusion on their faces.

"Forgive us, Your Highness," Cook said, bowing low. "You asked us to tell you what we knew of the Crimson Hoods. We only did as you asked."

"You told me stories and myths," Jeniah said. "I believed you."

"We only told you what Skonas asked us to tell you,"

Cook said. "He said it was for one of your lessons. We didn't know you were taking the stories so seriously. The truth about the Crimson Hoods is—"

Jeniah didn't let the old woman finish. She turned on her heel and went in search of her tutor. She found Skonas exactly where she'd left him in the library. He was pulling worms from a satchel and feeding them to Gerheart.

"Why did you do that?" she demanded, holding back tears. "You had everyone tell me lies, and you made me look like a fool. You're supposed to be my teacher."

"And what did you learn?" Skonas asked softly.

Jeniah stiffened. This was a lesson. One that was harsher and crueler than anything taught by any previous tutor. But, oh yes, she'd learned.

"To believe only that which I've seen or heard for myself," she said through bared teeth.

Skonas chuckled to himself. "It takes most people much longer to see that. You're learning your lessons quite swiftly. You might be *too* strangely clever for your own good."

"From now on, you are to tell me only the truth!"

"Everything I've said is the truth. *Somebody's* truth. Funny how truth changes, depending on who says it."

Too angry to speak, Jeniah turned and walked quickly to the door. But she couldn't give him the last word. Whirling around, she said, "Truth shouldn't be flexible!"

The tutor didn't even look at the princess when he responded. "People should be."

Walking back to her bedchambers, still shaking with anger, Jeniah made a vow: There would be no more lessons with Skonas. If she was to learn to be queen, she would do it on her own.

When she slept that night, Jeniah dreamt that she was searching through Emberfell at midnight with a blue-light lantern. The town had been abandoned. In the distance, the war horn pierced the night, dissonant and warbling. Out of the corner of her eye, she could see hooded figures lurking in every corner. But when she turned to face them, they vanished. She searched frantically as the lantern light grew dimmer and dimmer by the minute. When at last the light vanished, Jeniah had to concede.

She had no idea where Aon's father was.

Chapter Ten

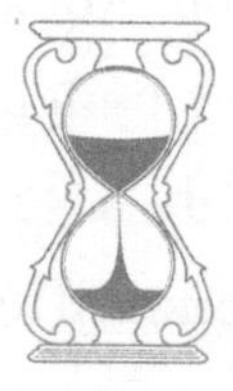

THE PEOPLE OF THE MONARCHY, OF COURSE, DID NOT HAVE BAD dreams. Such was the nature of their never-ending bliss. They all woke refreshed every morning, having dreamt only of honey-flavored tea and purple-tinted sunsets and everything that made them happy. They had no idea what a nightmare even was.

But Aon knew. Nightmares like the one where the mirebramble had overrun Emberfell, the vines pulling everything in their path toward the black marsh. Or the one where the Carse grew bigger and bigger before her eyes. From an early age, Aon found her nightmares told her what no one else knew about the black swamp. The Carse was what fierce things feared encountering in their own nightmares.

With Dreadwillow Carse on their right, Aon and Laius crept beneath the night's black canopy. Aon cast a glance toward Nine Towers. Was Jeniah in her room this very minute, waiting for word on what Aon had discovered? Was she pleading with the queen to release Aon's father and choose someone else to serve her? Yes. Aon had faith the princess was honoring their bargain. Now Aon had to find the strength to hold up her end.

The pair stopped at the entry to the Carse, framed by low-hanging dreadwillow branches. Laius was pale. Aon hadn't considered how the Carse would affect him while he waited. He kept eyeing the marsh and dancing in place. It was as if he *wanted* to be afraid but had no idea how. She pointed to a patch of grass across the road.

"Why don't you wait over there?" she said. "Farther away."

Laius didn't need to be told twice. He hugged the hourglass close to his chest and scurried to the clearing.

Aon clenched her teeth. She was used to the Carse's effects, but not immune. She nodded at Laius. "One hour."

Laius turned the hourglass upside down. Before she lost her nerve, Aon plunged into the Carse.

One . . . two . . . three . . .

She held her lantern out at arm's length. The bog was pitch-black during the brightest of days. It hardly seemed possible it could be darker at night. And it *wasn't* darker.

But it *was* creepier.

Twelve . . . thirteen . . . fourteen . . .

Every sound—the snapping of twigs beneath her feet, the breeze caressing the moss-laden tree branches—issued an ominous warning. Everything about this place had a single message: *Get out.*

It took all of Aon's concentration not to run from the Carse back to Laius. She focused on the image of her mother's face, the one she summoned each night before bed. She imagined what it would be like to be reunited with her father. Both tricks gave her the power to walk forward, inch by inch.

A twisting path of rounded earth served as the only way into the Carse. On either side of the winding trail, viscous ponds the color of tar burbled, spewing gray gas that mixed with the noxious mist all around. Aon held a damp cloth to her mouth to fend off the familiar stench of spoiled milk and olive juice. Fear coursed inside her like a ferocious summer gale, hot and relentless. She turned her head to listen hard for the singing. Yes, if she could just hear the song that filled her . . . But even that fervent wish couldn't distract her from the overwhelming urge to leave.

Aon reached into her pocket and clutched the royal crest she'd received from Jeniah. She drew strength from the thought that she was here on a mission from the princess.

It wasn't enough. Retreating from the Carse was more than an urge now. It was a need.

Why did I think I could do this? she asked herself. She'd tried over and over to explore the Carse. Entering in the name of the Queen Ascendant hadn't changed anything. It hadn't made her any braver. The crest hadn't given her Jeniah's immunity. She was doomed.

No! She stopped alongside the hook-shaped rock, unable to pass the imagined barrier. She ground her teeth, pushing back with what little will remained. All these dark thoughts. They didn't belong to her. The Carse was responsible. *This isn't my despair,* she reminded herself. *This isn't my despair.*

Once she realized this, she held her ground for the very first time. She couldn't move forward past the rock, but she didn't have to run. Aon smiled grimly at the darkness. "Stalemate," she whispered.

The slime ponds on either side of her path belched. Giant bubbles rose to the top of the mire and popped. Aon gripped the lantern tightly, preparing to use it as a weapon. She had to be ready for anything. She'd never seen the muck churn so violently.

She watched as something short and bulbous emerged, as if forming from the mud itself. The imp-like creature that stepped onto the path appeared to be made of wet clay and weedy flotsam, head and body in one misshapen sphere. It resembled a toad but was the size of a large dog. Its stubby, taloned feet—covered in black warts—pawed at the moist soil as it struggled to stand upright. It coughed repeatedly—the long, spindly arms on either side of its head flailing—until it spat a thick green liquid at Aon's feet.

A second, identical imp surfaced and joined its partner to block Aon's exit. The white-hot fear inside her chest threatened to explode as the creatures approached. She'd never seen anything like these beasts before. They looked like monsters from a fairy tale.

Both creatures gurgled and shook, their enormous eyes raking over every inch of Aon.

"She does not belong here," the first imp said.

Aon hadn't expected to hear the imps speak. She considered: if they could speak, could they also maybe . . . sing?

"Perhaps she was sent . . . ," the second imp mused.

"Yes," Aon said quickly, sensing an opportunity, "I was sent."

"As food," the second imp finished as a gob of saliva tumbled over its jaw and down its muddy chin.

The pair waddled slowly toward Aon, who backed up until she tripped on a root. She held up the royal crest.

"Look!" she said. "See? Do you know this?"

The imps immediately stopped, their lips drawing back in surprise.

"Oh," the first creature said. "The Highness."

"Yes," Aon said with a sigh of relief. "Princess Jeniah sent—"

"We have been expecting the Highness," the second creature said. It bent low in what Aon assumed was a bow. "We live to guide the Highness."

They think I'm the princess, Aon thought. Of the Monarchy's spare laws, there were probably punishments for pretending to be royalty. But going to a dungeon would be welcome if breaking the law kept her from being eaten.

She stood and squared her shoulders, as she imagined the real princess must do all the time. "I come here seeking information about the Carse."

The first creature's jowls quivered. "But of course, the Highness. Pirep only lives to serve."

Aon started at the name. She quickly composed herself when the imp eyed her suspiciously. "Pirep," Aon repeated with a nod. She turned to the second creature. "And you . . . You must be Tali?"

"Tali, the Highness," the second creature said with a croak. "Tali lives to serve. And eat. Tali lives to eat and serve."

It can't be, Aon thought. It was a coincidence. A very strange coincidence.

"If you know who I am," Aon said coolly, "then you know I am *not* to be eaten."

Both creatures shook their heads vigorously, sending flecks of spittle and slime in every direction. "Oh no, the Highness," Pirep said. "Pirep and Tali will guide and not eat."

"But maybe eat later," Tali muttered.

Pirep thumped Tali behind the ear. "No! No eating! Guiding!" Then Pirep waddled down the path. "Come, the Highness. Pirep knows just what to show."

Aon took a step forward, but no more. She tried to

follow, but foreboding held her back with the strength of steel chains. Her jaw trembled as she fought, but the feeling was too strong.

"I . . . can't," she gasped. "I can't go in any deeper."

Tali kicked at the ground. "Gots to pay the toll, she has. Highness or no!"

Aon's stomach fell. She hadn't thought to bring money. She pulled a tin brooch from her shirt. Her mother had made it for her. It had no monetary value, only that of a memory. But it was all she had to offer.

"Will you take this?" she asked.

Tali spat. "Shiny things? The Carse does not want shiny things."

Pirep tapped her foot impatiently. "The Highness is not knowing?"

At first, Aon was confused. *The Carse does not want shiny things.* How could the bog want *anything*? But then, she knew it was true. The Carse planted thoughts of terror in her head. If it was possible for the Carse to give, surely it could also take.

But what did it want? She thought of her previous visits to the Carse. The memory of how good it felt to pour out her grief roiled inside. Grief, later replaced with relief. Give and take.

Sadness. The Carse wanted sadness.

"I'm going to tell you a story," she said. "It's the story of a princess who was soon to become queen. You see, her mother was dying . . ."

Aon spun the story of Jeniah and her mother, being careful not to let on that she herself wasn't the princess. Aon described how Jeniah must have felt at the thought of losing her mother. It required little imagination.

As Aon wove the sad tale, the creatures began to sway. They closed their eyes and lay on the ground, sighing contentedly. The sadder the story became, the more these creatures grinned with their terrible, fat lips. They were enjoying it.

They were feeding off the misery.

Finishing the story, Aon came to understand something about the bog. Something she'd never known. The Carse wasn't just a place that evoked sadness. It *thrived* on gloom. That was why she felt so welcome here when she came to cry.

"The Highness is too good to Pirep and Tali," Pirep said, sighing with satisfaction.

And Aon realized she didn't feel terror anymore. Gingerly, she took a single step past the hook-shaped rock. Then another. And another. Nothing. No bone-chilling fear. No unrelenting desire to run. That was the secret to going in deeper. Sharing such profound misery had kept the effects of the Carse at bay. Aon had to laugh. That made her the only person in Emberfell who could *possibly* complete Jeniah's mission.

She knew she had to leave the Carse soon or Laius would alert the princess. "I'll return," she said to Pirep and Tali. "Will you guide me then?"

"We will always guide the Highness," Pirep said. With that, the twin creatures stepped from the path and disappeared back into the silty gray froth.

Aon ran down the path, back toward Emberfell. She felt renewed. For once in her life, the piece of her that was broken had proven useful. Her brokenness would be the key to giving Jeniah what she needed and getting her father back. And maybe, just maybe, learning the truth about her mother.

Here, sadness was a currency.

Here, Aon was wealthy.

Chapter Eleven

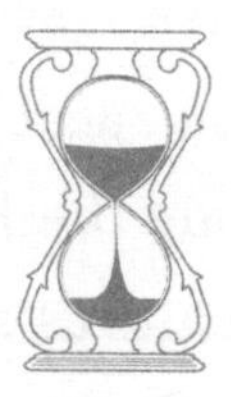

Your Royal Highness,

I have so much to share about my recent visit to Dreadwillow Carse! I don't know where to start.

Today, I ventured farther inside than I have ever gone before. What I saw during my time there was much as you would expect. In many ways, the Carse is a swamp, like any other.

And yet, it isn't. When you're inside the Carse, it's as if the swamp itself is trying to force you to leave by filling you with terror. I think this is meant to keep anyone from going to the very center of the Carse. Perhaps that is where I'll discover the secret you seek.

One strange thing I learned: I think the Carse is nourished by sadness. In fact, once I'd expressed sorrow, the terror lifted briefly, and I found it possible to go deeper in. But this doesn't make sense. There is no sadness to be found anywhere in the Monarchy. If the Carse requires sorrow to survive, how could it possibly exist and flourish? It's too big for my tears alone to sustain it. I hope to find the answer as I continue to explore for Your Highness.

I worry, though, that being in the Carse takes a toll. When I returned home, I collapsed. I recovered, but it may be a few more days before I feel strong enough to return. I promise to carry out your orders and learn everything I can.

Please know that you and your mother, the exalted Queen Sula, are in my thoughts. I pray you're both well and content.

Your obedient servant,

Aon

P.S. Throughout the Monarchy, the people tell the story of Pirep and Tali. Does Your Highness know this tale?

Dearest Aon,

I had no idea that being in the Carse for a long time would make you ill. Do whatever you need to recover.

Perhaps we should rethink this plan. Whatever secrets lie in the Carse are not worth exposing you to illness.

But you have definitely made me curious. Every monarch has worked tirelessly to ensure that people throughout the land are happy. If, as you say, the Carse needs sadness, how does it survive? If anything, it should be choking on the joy that surrounds it. Very strange.

I would ask my tutor, Skonas, but I doubt he would tell me. He is the most frustrating man I've ever met! He's supposed to be teaching me how to be a queen but his lessons are wrapped in half-truths and misdirection. I worry I won't learn what I need to know in time.

Thank you for asking of my mother's well-being. She has days when she sits up brightly and even sings softly to herself. Other days, she never leaves her bed. Her advisors perform more and more of her duties. But she remains committed to seeing her subjects happy and content.

Which raises a question: I have been told that sorrow is a royal privilege. You said that the only way you were able to proceed was by sharing your sorrow. How is this possible?

Her Royal Highness,

Jeniah, Queen Ascendant

P.S. I've never heard the story of Pirep and Tali. Is it a story of the Carse?

Your Royal Highness,

I promised you that I would learn the Carse's secrets, and I won't let you down. We don't need to rethink our plan. I will do as I said, knowing that my father's safe return relies on it.

Am I in trouble? I never meant to do something that was a royal privilege. The truth, Your Highness, is that I've always been able to feel sadness. I know I'm not supposed to. I can't help it. I've tried—so hard—to be as happy as everyone else in the Monarchy. I know that's what the queen wants. And I know it's what you will want when you become monarch.

If I could, I would take an oath right now to never again be sad. But if I made that vow, I'd break it. Not because I wanted to. Sadness is not a choice for me. It feels natural. I've hidden it very well. I don't know why I can't get rid of it like everyone else.

I will understand if you can no longer use me as your emissary. I will also understand if you have me arrested. No matter what you decide, I hope you can forgive me.

Your humble and obedient servant,

Aon

Dearest Aon,

Please know your father will be safely returned no matter what you discover in the Carse. When you put it that way, you make me feel like a scoundrel who is holding him hostage. Clearly, a mistake was made in his taking, and I will see that corrected. I only regret I have been unable to return him to you thus far. Things are a bit more complicated than I first thought. But know that I am trying to send him home to you.

As for feeling sorrow . . . You're right. The queen and I both want our people to be happy at all times. If anything, I worry that we have in some way failed you. I'm saddened that you know the burden of melancholy. Each day, Mother fades a little more, and now it feels like sadness is all I know.

But this just proves that you spoke the truth the night we met. You really are the only person who could possibly help me. If being able to express sorrow is required to explore the Carse, I need the one and only person besides me in the whole of the Monarchy who can do so. More than ever, dear Aon, I'm relying on you.

There is nothing to forgive. You remain my most trusted emissary.

You mentioned a story to me—about Pirep and Tali—but didn't explain why. What is the story? Is it important?

I would write more but I'm told my tutor is looking for me. I have no desire to see him, so I'm going to hide in the bathing chambers. Goodness knows he's never seen a bath. It's the last place he'll look!

Fondest wishes,

Jeniah

P.S. I would prefer if you addressed me as Jeniah. We are sisters, of a sort, sharing a great secret. I like the thought of having a sister.

Your Royal Highness,

You are too kind to forgive me. I admit, it's strange to share my sadness with someone. No one else knows this about me. My mother knew and she urged me to hide it. She said it would only cause problems if others knew. Imagine what she'd think if she found me talking about it with the Queen Ascendant!

I don't see sadness as a burden. I just see it as part of me. I only wish I knew why. It makes me different, and that is difficult. I feel broken.

Oh, the story of Pirep and Tali. I don't know if it's important or not. I suspect someone might be playing a trick on me. The story is hundreds of years old. It's about two girls who lived in Callowton, the town on the other side of the Carse from Emberfell. The two girls were wicked and often cried, feeling sad against the monarch's wishes. One day, they went into the Carse and were never seen again. Depending on who's telling the story, it sometimes ends with the Carse eating the girls.

Even though it's just a story, I've often wondered if there was some truth to it. Many years ago, my mother showed me our family tree. I learned that I had distant cousins whose names were Pirep and Tali. They lived about three hundred years ago. And there are no records of what happened to them. I'm starting to suspect it's not just a tall tale. I think Pirep and Tali might live in the Carse.

I'm sorry to hear your tutor is not helpful. I learned how to blow glass by watching my mother. Perhaps you could learn how to be queen by watching yours.

Your humble, obedient, and grateful servant,

Aon

P.S. I'm not sure I can call you by your first name. Not that I don't also feel like we're becoming sisters. But I want to show you how much I respect and love the Monarchy. You will always be "Your Royal Highness."

Dearest Aon,

You are brilliant! Yes, clearly I need to watch my

mother govern. That will tell me everything I need to know about being a queen. I've never watched her when she consults with her advisors. I've never been allowed. But surely they can't keep me out now, with so little time left. An excellent opportunity to watch her is coming up soon. Who needs Skonas? I can do this myself.

I'm embarrassed I didn't think of this myself. If you never learn anything useful about the Carse, I will forever be indebted to you for this. Many thanks!

Jeniah

P.S. Why do you feel Pirep and Tali live in the Carse?

Your Royal Highness,

Your mind is split in many directions, I would think. Your studies with your tutor, the queen's health, just to begin. I think that I might overlook such a simple solution, too, if I hadn't been able to concentrate. I'm glad I was of some small service.

As for Pirep and Tali, I'm not sure at all that what I encountered has anything to do with the story. The Carse is a strange place, and it may all have been a trick. Or maybe a test. Yes. I can't explain why, but every time I've ever entered the Carse, I felt it was testing me. This last time, more than ever.

I am recovering swiftly and plan to return to the Carse the night after next. I will report back when I learn more.

Your humble, obedient, grateful, and loyal servant,

Aon

Dearest Aon,

I am happy to hear you are on the mend. Please do not return to the Carse until you are fully well.

Since you first mentioned it, I haven't been able to get the story of Pirep and Tali out of my mind. I checked in the library and found several instances of the story. But none mentions that they went into the Carse. The storybooks all simply say the girls vanished.

I'm intrigued that you suspect these girls might be your distant relatives. If they were on your mother's side, would she know anything about them?

Jeniah

P.S. I really wish you'd call me Jeniah.

Your Royal Highness,

I don't know for sure that the girls who disappeared in the story are the same girls on our family tree. Maybe I will learn more when I'm in the Carse again.

Unfortunately, I cannot ask my mother. She's been gone for several years now.

Your humble, obedient, grateful, loyal, and devoted servant,

Aon

Dearest Aon,

I am so sorry to hear of your mother's passing. I think you know that I understand what you've been through.

Jeniah

Your Royal Highness,

Thank you, Your Highness, but my mother isn't dead.

Your humble, obedient, grateful, loyal, devoted, and dutiful servant,

Aon

Chapter Twelve

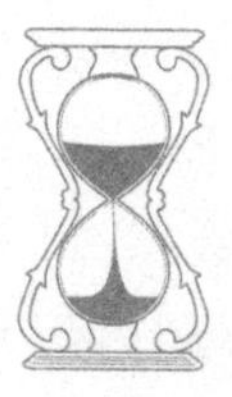

When the gigantic doors on the far side of the throne room swung wide and a line of finely dressed women and men walked in, a single thought entered Jeniah's mind: *At last!*

By custom, people from throughout the land gathered in the throne room at Judira Tower the last day of every week to petition the reigning monarch for assistance that only the royal family could give. Jeniah had decided to take Aon's advice to heart and announced to the royal staff that she would be joining the queen to hear this week's petitions. Watching her mother govern—*that* was how Jeniah would learn to be queen. For the first time, no one argued.

Hats in hands, the week's petitioners kept their eyes to the floor as they approached. Atop an oval dais, Queen Sula sat in a grand throne of gold and velvet, her head held high and a friendly if tight smile on her lips. In an alcove to her left, her most trusted advisors—scholars from every corner of the Monarchy—huddled together, ready to share their wisdom at the queen's request.

Jeniah sat to her mother's right on a smaller chair. It had been several days since the two had been this close. The princess could hear the queen laboring for each breath. All eyes fixed on the queen. Jeniah shifted in her seat and wondered what her mother was waiting for to start the proceedings.

A moment later, Skonas shambled into the room. Jeniah watched him strut past the petitioners as if *he* were their sovereign. All regarded him with a curious gaze but nodded politely in his direction. Skonas's gaze swept past Jeniah—not even sparing her a glance—and landed on the queen. He bowed and then moved to the far corner, where he picked at his furs as if looking for mites. He clicked his tongue when he found something and flicked it away in disgust.

With Skonas in place, the queen lifted her hand to start the petitions. One by one, the citizens of the Monarchy approached the dais.

"The summer was kind to me, Your Majesty," the first petitioner, a stout farmer with bushy eyebrows and a bushier beard, said. "I was gifted with the birth of many new cattle. But now I don't have enough grain to feed them."

The queen listened carefully to the man's plea. "I congratulate you on a plentiful year. You do the Monarchy credit. I grant you whatever grain you may need from the royal silos."

The next petitioner—a tall stick of a man with droopy shoulders—went to one knee before the throne. "Your Majesty," he said, "I am but a humble exchequer for the village of Bellshire. I am in love with the town's apothecary, but I worry I am not worthy of his affections. Do I dare tell him how I feel? Or should I seek a mate within my station?"

Queen Sula did not take a moment to consider. "The mate you seek should be the one who fills your heart," she said immediately. "Let no station in life create a barrier that dulls the joyful pleas of your deepest desires."

These were the petitions—the need for sage

advice—that worried Jeniah the most. When the queen spoke, it was with calming assurance. Everyone *knew* that what she said was true. How would Jeniah advise the people who asked for her help? Especially when the man who was supposed to be teaching her was currently in the corner, comparing the hairs in his beard to the furs on his chest.

Jeniah watched all morning as her mother carefully listened to each appeal, granted what was in her power to grant (which was nearly everything), and offered wisdom to those in need. Skonas cleared his gravelly throat when the final petitioner, a portly woman with a kind face, approached. The queen arched an eyebrow at the tutor and then gently touched her daughter's arm. "The Queen Ascendant will hear the final petition," the queen declared in a strong, clear voice.

Jeniah bit the insides of her cheeks. She wanted to decline. She wanted to cry. She didn't know what she'd say if the woman wanted advice on whether or not she should arrange a marriage between her son and the baker's daughter. She didn't have that sort of wisdom. As far as she knew, she didn't have *any* wisdom.

"Now that you are Queen Ascendant," the queen reminded her softly, "your word is law. Take your time. Measure your thoughts."

The petitioner bowed her head. Jeniah could feel the stares of everyone in the room. They inched over her flesh like scorpions searching for prey. *Please ask me for something I can grant,* Jeniah begged silently. *Wheat from our silos, sugar from our larder. Anything simple.* On the outside, she did as she'd watched her mother do since the first petitioner. She sat up straight, lifted her chin as if she'd done this a hundred times before, and nodded for the woman to begin.

"My family farms the orchards to the south of the river, Your Majesty—"

"No!"

Jeniah jumped at the sharp voice. All eyes turned to Skonas, who took a single step forward. "The proper address," he said icily, "is 'Your Highness.' Princess Jeniah cannot be addressed as 'Your Majesty' until she is truly a queen."

The farmer was startled by the sharp rebuke. Jeniah felt embarrassed for her. What Skonas had said was true, but the woman had made a simple mistake, surely not worthy of his hard tone. She glanced to see if her mother would scold the tutor. But the queen remained silent.

Jeniah turned back to the farmer and smiled. "Please continue," she said, and then added very pointedly, "There will be no more interruptions." The farmer composed herself and started again.

"As you know, Your Highness," the woman said, "every spring, we welcome the arrival of the ravens that nest in our orchards. They eat the insects and other vermin that would otherwise destroy the orchards' bountiful harvest of fruit. But this year, a small family of rubywings has taken to nesting in the orchards as well. Their bright color attracts predators that swoop in and eat the ravens. Because all in the Monarchy is yours, Queen Ascendant, we respectfully ask permission to protect the ravens."

Jeniah pretended to be considering very carefully. Really, she was trying not to throw up. She quietly drew air in between her teeth. She wanted to be fair. She glanced over to the queen's advisors, who stood at the ready. The queen had not once consulted them throughout the morning of requests. But surely she, the Queen Ascendant, could be allowed to ask others their advice, when she was so new at this.

"Reeve Ellsworth," the princess said, "what do you know of the rubywings?"

An elderly man with a balding pate stepped forward from the alcove. Each of the reeves was charged with having a thorough understanding of some aspect of the Monarchy. As Reeve of Nature, Ellsworth had knowledge second to none of all the plants and animals throughout the land.

"They are clever birds," the reeve said. "Once nested, they are not quick to move."

"Do you see a solution?"

The man nodded. "There are several ways to tend to the rubywings, Your Highness. Some are simple; others are difficult. Some are fast; some will take time."

"Such as?" Jeniah asked.

"Rubywings usually nest in Susurrus Valley," the reeve said. "Care could be taken to relocate this brood so they can be among their own kind. The valley's red-leafed trees will provide them shelter from predators."

"Or perhaps the rubywings could be sold," said Reeve Wane, the bright-faced woman who served as Reeve of Culture. "The milliners who live in the north keep rubywings as pets—they spoil them with fat worms and artesian water—and sometimes use their feathers in hat making."

Jeniah listened and nodded. "These are fair solutions," she said. Then she turned to the petitioner. "Do you agree?"

The woman seemed stunned that she was being consulted. "All I ask, Your Highness, is that the solution be expedient and executed with as little toil as possible so as not to disrupt the harvesting. Every day the rubywings live in the trees, ravens are dying and the harvest is in danger."

Jeniah watched her mother from the corner of her eye, searching for any sort of guidance. But the queen remained expressionless. Jeniah was on her own. Clearly, much was at stake. The plentiful ravens were dying. The trees' fruit would be ruined without the ravens to eat the insects that spoiled the harvest. Although it would inconvenience the rubywings to relocate them, it was clearly for the greater good.

The princess said to the farmer, "You may proceed as you see fit, doing whatever is swiftest and simplest to protect the ravens from being eaten."

The farmer thanked Jeniah. The queen's herald blew a horn, and the petitioners left.

"Let it be known," the queen whispered to her steward, "that this was the last audience I will grant. No more petitions will be heard until Jeniah is queen."

When the throne room had emptied, Jeniah kissed her mother good night and left for her own bedchambers.

"Tonight at sundown," Skonas said, appearing out of nowhere and falling into step at the princess's side, "I want you to go to Traithis Tower." Traithis was the second tallest spire after Lithe. It was used as a watchtower. Every window contained a telescope from which all corners of the Monarchy could be viewed. "Keep your eye on the orchards. You will see the people acting on the Queen Ascendant's will."

Something warm tickled Jeniah's stomach. She hadn't thought of that. She had made a royal declaration, and people were going to act on it. *Your word is law*, her mother had said. This would be the way of things from now on.

She could make a difference.

"And what did you think of your third lesson?" Skonas asked Jeniah.

Third lesson? Skonas hadn't said a word throughout the audience, except to correct the farmer. It hadn't even been his idea for her to observe the petitions. But when she thought about it, she *had* learned it was important to consider the needs of the multitudes over the needs of a handful. That would no doubt guide her in future petitions.

"I think," Jeniah said smoothly, "I should like more lessons like that."

Skonas chuckled. "Perhaps someday someone will do that for you. But remember, I promised you just three lessons. You will set the fourth and final lesson yourself. I will stay only until you have finished."

The tutor nodded respectfully; then he turned and made for the tower's exit.

At sundown, Jeniah went to the top of Traithis Tower as Skonas had instructed. She turned the largest telescope to the south until the lens fell on the orchards.

She watched as a slim man approached the largest tree with ginger steps. He raised a pole and tapped it fiercely on the lower branches.

The orchard seemed to explode. What Jeniah had believed to be a thicket of leaves was, in reality, a flock of ravens that burst forward from the tree's bare branches. The sky filled with the black birds, blotting out the glowing horizon like a funeral shroud.

In the turmoil of birds flying everywhere, Jeniah spotted four flashes of scarlet. The rubywings, which looked exactly like the ravens but for the shiny red feathers on their wings, raced to keep up with their darker brethren.

And just as quickly as they'd taken flight, the rubywings fell to the ground, one by one. Jeniah gasped. She twisted the end of the telescope, and the distant image came into sharper focus. The birds lay at the base of the tree, a single arrow through each of their chests. The ravens continued on untouched until they became one with the night sky.

Four archers emerged from the nearby bushes, clapping one another on the back and sharing congratulations on their marksmanship. The queen's advisors had said there were several options. They hadn't mentioned that one option—the one the farmer had chosen—was killing the birds.

"That's not what I meant," Jeniah whispered.

But it's what she'd said. She'd given the woman permission to take care of the problem, and that was what the woman had done. She'd sacrificed a few rubywings for the many ravens in the name of doing what was easiest.

The assurance Jeniah had felt earlier—the knowledge that she had done the right thing—slipped away. Now, she was afraid. She didn't want to speak ever again. The power she wielded was too much. For once, she saw just how much what she said mattered.

Your word is law.

Chapter Thirteen

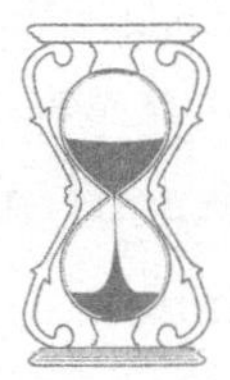

AON LAY IN BED AND LISTENED TO A DISTANT ROOSTER CROW FOR the third time. She'd been awake since long before sunup. Today, she'd decided, she would return to the Carse. She'd spent the past week shaking off the effects that had lingered since her last visit. This had never happened before.

When she'd first emerged from the bog to find Laius eyeing the hourglass—its final sands trickling away—she'd taken a deep breath. Inside the Carse, the fear always filled her like something liquid and heavy. It weighed her down. Once she was outside, the heaviness drained away, and the fear vanished. She'd waited for this to happen. The fear vanished, as always. The weight did not.

For the next few days, Aon still felt that heavy weight pulling at her arms and legs and head like leaden marionette strings. Every move she made was slow and labored. And all the more curious was the nagging sensation that it was *familiar.* Like she was still in the bog and yet wasn't. Almost as if she'd taken a part of the Carse with her.

Or maybe left a bit of herself behind.

For the first couple days, Mrs. Grandwyn mistook Aon's symptoms for the flu and confined the girl to bed. Mrs. Grandwyn cheerily served chicken soup and reminded Aon to keep her head high because all illnesses passed. For the better part of a week, Aon was convinced this feeling would never pass.

But it did. Just this morning, she finally felt like the weight was no longer tugging at her. For the first time since her return, she felt back to normal. Which proved to be a whole new problem. She missed the weight. She *craved* it. She hadn't realized it—she had been too worried about the weight lingering—but when the heaviness was inside her, Aon hadn't felt broken. The idea of returning to the Carse so she could feel that way again filled her with excitement.

Late that night, Aon and Laius slipped from the house with the hourglass. Aon had lent it to her stepbrother so he could stare at it when he practiced blowing glass each morning. Now he carried it with him wherever he went, pleased to be entrusted with something that he knew meant so much to Aon. At one with the shadows, Aon and Laius made their way to the entrance of the Carse.

"Two turns?" Laius asked. If the boy had a problem with Aon spending that much time in the bog, his ability to express it was limited to a lopsided grin and crinkled brow.

Aon nodded. "Two hours this time." When she saw how unsure Laius seemed, she added, "Don't worry. I won't be alone." She didn't know if she could trust Pirep and Tali. They seemed just as willing to eat her as help her. But then, they'd given her the secret to warding off the Carse's effects. As long as she could continue to express her sadness, she could travel anywhere in the dark bog.

Laius took his place across the road from the Carse's entrance, nodded, and gave the hourglass its first turn. With the sands trickling down, and eagerness practically prodding her every step, Aon returned to the Carse.

Immediately, she felt that familiar weight. Her arms drooped at her sides, and her stride was sluggish. And she loved it. She felt the fear, but it wasn't nearly as strong as it had been. Which seemed suspicious. She ventured forward, on her guard.

Aon's thoughts strayed to Jeniah. There were things she hadn't told the princess in her letters. Like how she'd shared the story of the princess and the dying queen. Or that she'd met creatures who shared names with two fabled cousins. Or how she'd allowed her implike guides to believe that she, Aon, was Jeniah. *These details aren't important*, Aon had reasoned while writing the letters. *She wants to know what is keeping her from the Carse. Why bother her with things that don't matter?*

But now, back in the Carse, she felt ashamed about the omissions. Jeniah had been nothing but honest with her from the start. Aon was a traitor. Not only to the princess but to all the Monarchy. She wasn't worthy of the royal family's trust. She was nothing but a liar. She wanted to give up right now . . .

Aon clenched her jaw and marched forward. Another new trick of the Carse. Guilty feelings had almost succeeded in making her abandon her charge. Almost.

She had to smile: she'd forced the Carse to change how it dealt with her. Which meant she was winning.

Aon returned to the hook-shaped rock. As if they knew she was coming, the imps emerged from the sludge and led the girl onward. "What does the Highness want to know?" Pirep asked.

"There is an ancient warning," Aon said. "It states that no monarch can enter the Carse, or else the Monarchy will fall."

"The Highness is here," Tali said. "Has the Monarchy fallen?"

Aon ignored the question. "I wish to understand what the warning means. I believe the answer lies somewhere in the Carse."

Pirep gave an odd little croak that Aon thought *might* have been a chuckle. "Many answers lie in the heart of the Carse," Pirep said. "Answers to questions no one asks."

Tali clawed at the ground. "What does the Highness fear more? The answers or the questions?"

Aon fixed the imps with a confident stare. "I fear neither."

The imps burbled at each other, saying words Aon didn't understand. Then they turned and trod deeper into the Carse, motioning for Aon to follow. She fell into step behind them.

The trio wended its way around massive tree roots that arced up out of the ground. Aon held her nose as the pungent odors grew worse. Now she could smell hot tar and rotting meat. None of it affected Pirep and Tali. They traipsed ahead without a care in the world.

As their path curved to the left, Aon stopped to find a massive boulder blocking the way. The imps quickly scaled the rock, going up and over without a second thought. Aon eased her way around, only to discover other rocks strewn about, some half-sunk in the mire, others piled one atop another as if aspiring to climb up out of the darkness. She hadn't seen stones like this anywhere else in the Carse. Where had they come from?

As Aon made her way back to the path, the answer became clearer. Ahead was a wooden-framed doorway wrapped in moldy ivy. It dripped ooze and looked ready to collapse onto the stony ground that held it up. But it was most certainly a doorway.

"What is this place?" Aon asked.

"The first monarch," Pirep said. "Before Nine Towers, the first monarch lived here. A mighty castle."

Aon surveyed the mounds of shattered gray stone.

If there was a castle to be seen, it existed only in Pirep's imagination. Peering through the curtain of fog, Aon could just make out the mangled, rusted web of metal that remained of a once-great portcullis alongside the crumbling doorway.

Aon had known nothing of a castle that came before Nine Towers. But if the royal family had once lived behind these fallen walls, there was a chance she'd learn what she needed here.

Straight ahead, the ruins of a turret jutted up out of the swamp like a malformed fang. Aon watched as a wisp of gray light emerged from the ever-present vapor near the top of the fallen tower. The light took the shape of a transparent man, tall and thin. The man, who wore a crown with nine points, stepped from the turret onto a decaying balcony. He looked out into the Carse, and then bowed his head and silently wept.

A second later, the light winked from existence. Then the scene repeated: the man formed inside the turret, stepped onto the precipice, and wept. This happened over and over.

Aon pressed her hand against an archway to steady herself. "Is that . . . Is that a ghost?"

Tali spat. "No ghosts! No such thing. Shades. Shades in the Carse. Nothing but shades."

When Aon moved to get a closer look, a flicker of light caught her attention. She turned to see more shades near a pile of broken timber and chains that might once have been a drawbridge. The shades wore armor emblazoned with the royal crest, signifying the monarch's personal army. They loaded and fired a catapult aimed at the castle, and then did it again. Over and over, like the shade in the turret.

Aon saw the faces of the shades and gasped. These soldiers launched their ghostly assault with wide smiles.

"What's going on here?" Aon asked. But it seemed clear.

Insurrection. The king's own soldiers—who had no doubt sworn a blood oath to protect their liege at all costs—had once attempted to overthrow him. Aon had studied the history of the Monarchy, but this was one fact she'd never learned. A revolution should be worthy of at least a footnote.

"King Isaar," Pirep explained, pointing back to the turret. "The Just Ruler, they called him. The Peace Bringer. The Mad Monarch."

Aon whirled around. "Mad? What do you mean 'mad'?" This was another fact missing from the history books. Isaar had only ever been referred to with awe. No book had ever called him mad.

Tali scaled the remains of a balustrade. The creature's stubby arm indicated the entirety of the castle ruins. "He stayed inside. Trebuchets! Battering rams! Siege engines! All laid waste to his home."

A picture of the king formed in Aon's mind. She could see him valiantly defending his homestead from usurpers in the name of the Monarchy he'd helped forge. "How was that mad?"

Pirep made a guttural sound, a mix between a sigh and a sob. "Isaar ordered them to attack. No one knew he was inside."

The shade of King Isaar returned to the precipice again. Now that she was closer, Aon could see deep lines marking the monarch's face. Her mother's face had looked like that. *Worry lines*, she'd called them. From the look of King Isaar, Aon suspected he had experienced every worry ever known.

"Why?" Aon asked. "Why would he do that?"

Tali belched. "Because he was *mad*!"

So, it wasn't insurrection. Isaar had ordered the castle destroyed. The soldiers were following orders, not knowing their king was inside. This could be why the princess had been forbidden from entering the Carse. To prevent her from learning about her mad ancestor. But it didn't seem likely. How would the entire Monarchy fall at the discovery?

"King Isaar," Pirep said. "He is why we have a Carse."

Aon shuddered. "What does that mean?"

The imp was about to reply, but then stopped and squinted up at Aon. "Is the Highness unwell? The Highness looks unwell."

It took the question to make Aon realize she *wasn't* feeling well. Her hands had gone clammy, and her temples throbbed. This was the longest she'd ever spent inside the Carse. The longest *anyone* had spent inside, as far as she knew. It occurred to her that maybe it was unwise to stay much longer.

"I—I think I have to go," Aon said. She stumbled backward. The fear and guilt were gone. Now she felt only befuddled. Another trick of the Carse. "How long have we been here?"

She'd always had a good sense of time. She'd made her way out of the swamp before in just under an hour. But suddenly, she found herself less sure how long it had been.

Pirep belched. "Hard to tell. Time, in the Carse."

"I should go," Aon said, rubbing her hands. They had started to itch.

"Much to learn here, the Highness," Pirep called to her. "Many answers for you in the Carse. Many, many answers."

She's trying to get me to stay, Aon thought. If she was going to continue searching the Carse, she needed to find a way to beat this latest trick.

She made her way through the wooden archway and paused to steady herself. Her fingers grazed a notch, and when she examined it, she found several curved lines etched into the rotting wood.

A rose blossom.

Aon swallowed hard. Her mother had etched that symbol into every piece of glass she'd ever blown. This rose matched all the others precisely, like a signature. Its presence on the door frame could mean only one thing: her mother had been here. Years ago, clearly. The etching was weathered. But her mother had made it this far in. Aon gently pressed her fingertips into the blossom's grooves. She closed her eyes and choked back a sob. *You left this for me*, she thought. *A message. I'm on the right track . . .*

The brief moment of clarity faded as confusion clouded Aon's mind. A wave of dizziness overcame her. Using all her effort to focus, Aon made her way out toward the path that led from the Carse. She repeated the details she'd learned at the castle ruins over and over, wanting to get them exactly right when she wrote to Jeniah.

I'm here to help the princess, she reminded herself with each step. *If I find what the princess needs, she can return Father. That's why I'm here.*

Aon thrust the lantern out in front of her to light the path. As she did, she caught a glimpse of her hand. Her fingers had become wrinkled and gray. Black warts covered each knuckle.

Aon picked up the pace. She suddenly understood why she no longer felt fear or guilt. The bog had changed tactics yet again. She now knew what became of anyone who remained inside too long. She also now understood what had happened to Pirep and Tali. If Aon stayed too long, she would become like the imps.

The Carse was sending her a message: if it couldn't scare her away, it would claim her.

Chapter Fourteen

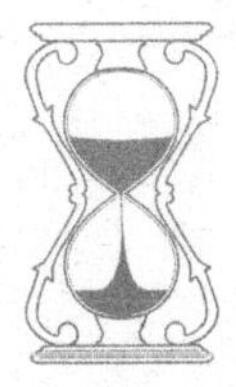

Your Royal Highness,

I have returned from my second trip into the Carse and have much to tell you. With this letter, I'm sending several more pages that describe everything I saw. I don't know if any of it explains why you're forbidden from entering the Carse, or why the Monarchy would fall if you did, but what I've seen suggests that the answer is somewhere in that swamp. It's only a matter of time before I find it.

In my report, I mention the strange creatures who have been guiding me. They're unlike any animal I know. They never leave my side. And yet, I always have the feeling that even if they left, I still wouldn't be alone.

I plan to return again soon to continue searching for answers.

Can you please tell me when I can expect my father to come home? Every morning, I wake, hoping to see him back at our house.

Your obedient servant,

Aon

Dearest Aon,

I have read through your description several times now. I cannot thank you enough for sending it to me. This isn't anything like I imagined the Carse would be. Imps made of mud and clay. The ruins of an old castle. The shade of King Isaar. I can't believe the king ordered an attack on his castle while he was still inside. I've studied the history of my ancestors, and nothing *even suggests that happened to Isaar.*

I agree that nothing you've learned explains why I am not allowed into the Carse. Thank you for continuing to explore. I am confident you'll find the answer soon.

And now, I have to confess. It pains me to say this, Aon, but I don't know where your father is. I'm so sorry. When you first told me about the Crimson Hoods, I assumed they were a secret kept by my mother. I agreed to return your father, thinking I would simply be able to ask my mother for his release. But my mother claims the Crimson Hoods are a myth.

I swear on my crown that I will find out what is happening. I fear some rogues may be kidnapping people in my mother's name. Or perhaps there's an even more sinister explanation. I've long suspected that magic might actually be real. It would explain how mysterious these Hoods are, coming only during the gloamingtides and never speaking. If it's true that the Hoods are magical, it's even more urgent that we track them down.

Could you please tell me more about what you know of these Hoods? I need a clue to begin looking for an answer.

Again, I apologize that I didn't tell you sooner. But I'll make this right. It is the monarch's duty to protect the people, and I would be a terrible queen if I couldn't do that for your father.

Your friend,

Jeniah

Your Royal Highness,

I can't believe what you've said. All my life, I was raised to believe the Crimson Hoods served the queen.

That the chosen few served her in Nine Towers. It was all a lie. Why would someone do this?

Please, Your Highness, I beg you to find him! He has had an injury since birth that makes it difficult for him to walk. Why would someone take a wounded man?

The Crimson Hoods are not a myth. They have been a part of our lives for as long as anyone can remember. We sing songs about them at the gloamingtide festival. Everyone dreams of being taken by them to serve the monarch. I will do whatever it takes to help. My father is all I have left.

I know that our pact is secret. I won't tell anyone what I do for you in the Carse. But if you come to Emberfell, you can speak to anyone, and they'll tell you the Crimson Hoods are real.

That night we met, I told you everything I knew about the Hoods. My new mother, Mrs. Grandwyn, knows much more of our history than I do. She could tell you all you need to know. Please, Your Highness, come talk to her.

Your servant,

Aon

Your Royal Highness,

It's strange for this much time to pass between our letters. Usually, when I write, I can expect your response within a day (sometimes sooner). It has been three days now, and I have yet to hear from you. I have a list of people who are willing to tell you about the Crimson Hoods. All you need do is consent to visit. Again, I promise not to tell anyone about our business in the Carse. But if it means finding my father, I think it's important you know everything about the Hoods. Please respond.

Your servant,

Aon

Dearest Aon,

I'm afraid it won't be possible for me to come to Emberfell. My mother has taken a turn for the worse and grows weaker by the hour. I don't feel I can leave Nine Towers.

She's going to die soon, Aon. She's going to die soon, and I still don't know how to be queen. The monarch defends the peace and prosperity. If I don't know how to do that, what will happen to that peace? I could destroy the Monarchy without ever setting foot in that wretched Carse.

I don't know what to do.

Jeniah

Chapter Fifteen

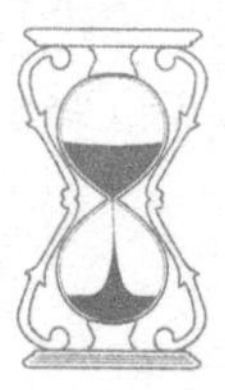

NOT EVEN THE HALLS OF RAVUS TOWER, THE MOST FORTIFIED IN the castle, could keep out the autumn chill. Jeniah would remember that nip in the air for the rest of her life. It was only a short walk from her own bedchambers to her mother's, but the trip—taken with soft, hesitant steps—seemed to last forever. And the cold was her only companion.

Jeniah thought of Aon. In that moment, she wanted nothing more than to talk to the girl from Emberfell—that strange, wonderful girl who might possibly be the only person able to understand what she was feeling.

The servants in Nine Towers had always done their best to help Jeniah when she was sad. But people who understood only happiness could do only so much to ease Jeniah's pain.

She paused outside the door to her mother's bedchambers as she had every day since the Chief Healer had delivered the news of the queen's worsening condition. The information had come with the gentle suggestion that the princess spend as much time with her mother as possible over the coming hours.

And then he'd said those words. Those terrible, awful words she'd always known he would say to her one day.

It won't be long now.

Jeniah pushed open the door. The odor of rose water and mint salve nearly overpowered her. There was a time when just the hint of that salve made her smile; it smelled like her mother. Now, however, Jeniah linked the scents to her growing despair. She never wanted to smell them again.

She glided softly to her mother's side. Queen Sula's dark skin glistened with a feverish sweat. Her lips were chalky, and her puffy eyes stared blankly ahead. The princess almost ran from the room, unable to bear the sight. *She is still your mother*, she reminded herself. *And she needs you.* The queen wheezed and stirred, and then patted her bedside.

Jeniah sat on the mattress and took her mother's hand. "They said you'd live a month."

"They said I'd live a month at most," the queen rasped. "They never discussed how short my time could be."

"It's not fair," Jeniah said, and then she looked away, ashamed. She'd tried so hard never to utter those words. She felt childish and weak.

Queen Sula reached up and turned her daughter's face so they could speak eye to eye. "It's all right to think that. It's all right to think anything you want right now. Be angry at me. Be angry at the sickness. Be angry at everything and everyone. There are no wrong feelings. Do what you need to do."

Jeniah *did* feel angry at everything and everyone. But she didn't want to waste what time they had left feeling that way. "It's too much. I can't even think about becoming queen while you're confined to bed. I won't leave your side."

All at once, it occurred to her. She'd been selfish and silly trying to learn more about the Carse. She would send for Aon at once and stop her trips into the bog. She would do what her mother and every monarch before her had done and ignore that accursed place. The longer she thought about it, the more she realized: it was the only thing required of her to be a good queen. It was really that simple.

But it wasn't.

The queen took her daughter's hand, the opal rings they each wore touching as she did. "There will be days to mourn me. Days and nights and weeks and months and whatever time you feel you need. But you're mourning me while I'm still here. Use this time. Talk to me."

It was hard for Jeniah to banish her sadness. She was first a daughter whose mother was dying and second an heir to the throne. But she needed so many answers. Her mother was right. She had to grieve *and* rule. For now.

"The ancient warning says the Monarchy will fall if I enter Dreadwillow Carse. Does that mean that if I never go there, the Monarchy will never fall?"

"I'm afraid there's more to ruling than giving the Carse a wide berth," her mother said, a small smile passing across her pain-racked face. "As queen, you must still provide counsel and guidance for the good of all."

Tears welled in Jeniah's eyes. "Mother, they killed

the rubywings. I never told them to do that, but that was what they chose because it was quick and easy. And I told them it was fine. It was my fault."

"Painful as it is, sometimes we learn by failure. I lost count of the number of lessons I've learned that way, and—"

"But I hate that!" Jeniah burst out. "So many people will rely on me soon, and I don't know how to lead them. Why aren't *you* teaching me how to be queen?"

The queen reached out her shaking hand and laid it on Jeniah's arm. "Why do you think that would help?"

"You're a good queen. Everyone says so. You know everything."

"Jeniah, I can't tell you how to be queen. I can only tell you how *I* was queen. That's very different."

"But that's what I want. To be just like you."

"Are you unhappy with Skonas?"

Jeniah held back a fiery desire to tell her mother *exactly* what she thought of her tutor. *He's cruel, sneaky, untrustworthy, and arrogant*, she thought. Instead, she only frowned. "I don't always understand what he wants me to learn."

"Good," the queen said. "It's nice to hear some things never change."

"But he doesn't tell me anything. I ask a question, he asks a question in return. I don't think I'll ever learn anything from him."

"Skonas will show you where to look for answers," the queen said, "but he won't tell you what to see."

"And that will help me be queen?" It didn't seem possible.

Her mother nodded. "He taught me, you know. He's been teaching monarchs for a very, very long time."

Jeniah blinked. How could that be? Clearly, Skonas was much older than he appeared. "Who is this man? Where is he from?" *And how*, she thought, as a new idea formed, *can he feel something other than happy?* The only other person she knew who could do that, aside from royalty, was Aon.

"Think about what you already know of him," the queen prompted.

"He said he wasn't a royal subject," Jeniah drawled slowly, trying to make sense of this. "He said I have no power over him."

"There are almost no limits to the power of the Monarchy. But, yes, Skonas is beyond those limits. He is here out of kindness."

"His kindness is hurting the Monarchy! He's taking

too long to teach me what I need to know. If I had to take the throne tomorrow, I couldn't." Jeniah trembled, the very thought of assuming her reign the next day paralyzing her. Queen Sula wrapped her thin arms around her daughter and pulled her close.

"I will tell you this much," the queen said, stroking Jeniah's long, sable hair. "I believe you already know everything you need to be queen. You just don't realize it yet. That's why Skonas is here. He'll help you see what's already there."

"But I'm so afraid of doing the wrong thing. If you won't tell me what to do, tell me what *not* to do. So many people count on me. I don't want to make mistakes."

"There is only one way to ensure you never make a mistake."

"What's that?"

"Do nothing."

Jeniah thought about it. If she'd done nothing, the rubywings would still be alive. But then, the ravens would still be hunted by predators. "But what if doing nothing is a mistake?"

The queen closed her eyes, a light smile returning to her lips. Her words slid from between her teeth like a whispered dream. "Skonas is right. You *are* strangely clever."

Before Jeniah could respond, the queen was asleep. The princess watched her mother's chest rise and fall, just enough to keep her alive. Jeniah made wishes. She uttered prayers. Then she kissed her mother's forehead and tiptoed out of the bedchambers.

It wasn't until she'd closed the door behind her that it struck Jeniah: her mother hadn't answered the question about why Skonas instead of the queen was teaching her. In fact, the queen had answered that question . . . with another question.

UNABLE TO SLEEP that night, Jeniah holed herself up in the library. The ancient tomes may not have had much to say about the Carse, but they held much knowledge about her family's history.

King Isaar is why we have a Carse. That was what the creatures Aon had described in her letter had said. But what did it mean? Jeniah could picture King Isaar, the first monarch. His portrait was the largest in the Grand Hall. It was the first one you noticed when you entered.

When she was younger, Jeniah had feared old King Isaar. He had a long, careworn face with a goatee that ended in a sharp point. His eyebrows arched, challenging all who dared look. At times, Jeniah swore his harsh eyes followed her wherever she went into the room.

"Why does he always look so angry?" Jeniah had once asked her mother.

Queen Sula had laughed and said, "King Isaar loved this land more than anyone else. What you see as anger, others would see as fatherly concern."

At the time, Jeniah's father had still been alive. *His* fatherly concern never looked angry. Jeniah thought her mother was wrong about King Isaar. But as frightening as she found the old king, it made no sense to Jeniah that a monarch would create a place his descendants were forbidden to enter.

Jeniah thought about the castle ruins Aon had described. She'd never heard of her ancestors living anywhere but Nine Towers. And why was the Carse located on the old castle's grounds? Surely the history books would offer an explanation.

But they didn't. As before, when she'd gone looking for information on the Carse, Jeniah read every history book until her eyes watered. There was no mention of an old castle. Jeniah was starting to suspect that someone had gone to great lengths to rewrite her family's history.

Jeniah flung the nearest book across the room. As hard as she tried, she could think of no way to see—

To *see* where the old castle had stood.

A royal dwelling would have been a landmark. The sort that appeared on maps.

Every one hundred years, the royal cartographer was charged with updating the official maps of the Monarchy. The history books may not have mentioned the Carse. But the maps definitely would.

Jeniah left the mounds of books behind and burrowed through the cartographer's archives, collecting every map and laying them all out side by side on the floor. She started with the very first map, the one ordered by King Isaar when he created the Monarchy. She had to squint, but there it was: the Carse was nothing more than a pinprick to the right of center on the map, its name scrawled in such tiny print as to make it nearly invisible. And there was the royal family's first castle.

The next map, drawn a hundred years later, was the first to show Nine Towers. It, too, depicted the Carse. But now it was a small circle, the size of her thumbnail. The old castle was gone.

Jeniah walked along the path of maps, showing one thousand years of history. Something cold and unyielding blossomed in her chest with each step. The maps told a story, a story that perhaps no one else had ever seen. Unless, of course, someone viewed all the maps at once as Jeniah was doing.

The Carse was growing.

Each map showed the black spot had doubled—sometimes tripled—in size during the hundred years since the last map was drawn. Jeniah quickly did the sums in her head. At the rate the Carse was growing, it would overtake Emberfell in the next hundred years. And Nine Towers in the century after that, if not sooner. If it continued to grow, it would eventually engulf the entire Monarchy.

Jeniah ran from the library. She had to write Aon immediately to tell her what she'd learned. But as she returned to Ravus Tower, she barreled into the Chief Healer coming from the queen's bedchambers. Jeniah's arms went limp when she saw the look in the healer's eyes.

"The queen has fallen into a deep slumber," the Chief Healer said, his hand gently squeezing the princess's shoulder. Jeniah had been told this might happen, and she knew what it meant.

The chances of the queen's ever awakening were very slim.

Chapter Sixteen

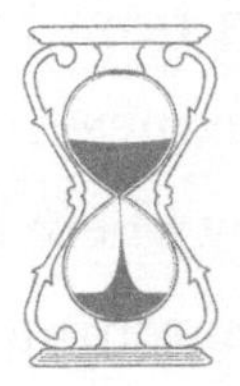

It took three days for Aon's hands to return to normal.

Since returning from the Carse, she'd worn gloves everywhere to avoid explaining what had happened. She could only hope it wasn't permanent. And, thankfully, over time, the warts fell off, and her skin returned to its pink, fleshy color. But the heaviness inside her remained.

In the time it took to recover, Aon realized she'd made a mistake. The Carse had ceased to have power over her once she'd shared her misery. But in doing so, she'd allowed the Carse inside her.

And it showed no signs of leaving.

When several days passed and she hadn't heard back from the princess, Aon started writing another letter. She'd planned to explain to Jeniah that she was very sorry, but she couldn't continue searching the Carse. She had no idea how long she could stay inside the Carse before she was fully an imp. Five hours? Four? Less? She couldn't take the chance. And now that Aon knew the princess didn't know where her father was, her time would be better spent searching for him herself.

Then Jeniah finally replied.

I could destroy the Monarchy without ever setting foot in that wretched Carse.

And with that, Aon remembered what was at stake: the entire Monarchy. As worried as she was about her father's fate, he was one man compared to every living soul under the monarch's care. If Jeniah did something to shatter the peace and prosperity of the Monarchy, Aon would share the blame. She was in a position to help the princess and prevent catastrophe. Finding her father had to wait. She *had* to return to the bog. If she didn't, she was doing exactly what the Carse wanted.

As everyone in Emberfell slept, Aon packed a small hourglass to take with her into the Carse. Then she and Laius slipped away as they had before.

"Three turns tonight, Laius," she instructed once they'd reached the entrance of the Carse.

The boy nodded dutifully. "Three." More than ever, Aon wished Laius could feel something other than happy. She wanted to know that *someone* was as afraid for her as she was for herself.

I'll stay as long as I can, Aon told herself. *I'll watch for signs. If I start to change, I'll get out at once.* At least, that was the plan.

She nodded to Laius. Aon took out her own hourglass and together, she and Laius turned them upside down. Aon prayed softly that this would be the last time they ever needed to do this.

THE IMPS WERE waiting for Aon at the hook-shaped rock. As always, they bowed low before leading Aon onward. Aon found herself coaxing them along, wanting to get farther in tonight than they'd ever taken her before. But the creatures' small legs could go only so fast.

They traveled past the castle ruins, trudged through a stream of ankle-deep silt, and scaled a small crag of slick stone. All the while, Aon kept an eye on the small hourglass that hung from a chain on her waist. When the sands ran out, she gave it a turn. One hour down.

The imps began leapfrogging over each other,

leading Aon on until they reached a mist-filled oasis. Before them, a still pond, shaped like an eye, interrupted the path.

"Welcome!" Pirep said before diving into the pool of muck and wallowing about. "Welcome to the garden."

The Carse seemed like an odd place for a garden. But then, the garden itself was odd.

Topiaries, twisting and bent, rose up out of the mire on either side of the path. The low-hanging branches of the dreadwillow trees were covered with newly bloomed flowers. When Aon leaned over to smell the blossoms, their transparent petals shrunk away and curled up until the flowers looked like claws.

The imps draped sinewy weeds around their heads, like regal laurels, and escorted Aon farther.

Aon reached out and brushed her fingers against the nearest topiary. A slimy patina of moss and algae fell away, revealing a gnarled, gray-white branch. When Aon inspected it more closely, her mouth went dry.

The topiaries were made from bones.

Hundreds and hundreds of bones had been piled up and fused together into macabre sculptures.

"What is this place?" Aon whispered.

Tali nestled up to a topiary, her short arms reaching out as if to embrace it. "Told you. A garden."

Aon shook her head. "But it must be more than that."

"Now a garden," Pirep said, gesturing ahead. "Then a battlefield."

Aon moved to where the imp was pointing and spotted a small island in the middle of a pool of muck. In the center of the island stood a tall stone obelisk. She waded through the mire until she was close enough to sec hundreds—no, thousands—of names etched up and down the side.

"It's a war memorial," she said in disbelief.

The idea seemed absurd to Aon. No one alive in the Monarchy had ever known war. War was a myth about faraway lands, told so everyone would better appreciate the peace of the Monarchy. But then, Aon was discovering that truth and fiction had more in common for her lately. She gazed at the monuments of bone all around. Was this what the princess wasn't meant to know?

Climbing up, Aon moved onto the small island. Fog rolled in from the densest part of the forest and twinkled with pale gray light. At the base of the cenotaph, the ghostly outlines of two shades, deep in a silent conversation, took shape.

The first shade Aon recognized immediately. It was a young King Isaar, robust and healthy, nothing like the shade of the mad king under siege at the castle ruins.

Isaar spoke to a second man wearing fine clothes and a neatly trimmed beard. Severely angled eyebrows gave his eyes a shifty look. The stranger listened carefully as Isaar spoke and nodded occasionally. Isaar held out his hand. The stranger paused, looking suddenly unsure. Then, shoulders slumped, the stranger reached out and shook the king's hand. The shades flickered away, only to re-form a moment later and repeat their conversation.

"Who is the man with King Isaar?" Aon called over her shoulder to the imps, who were now pelting each other with patties of mud and grass.

"He has many names," Tali called back, gargling on swamp water. "Many, many names."

"Many names throughout a life," Pirep added.

Aon frowned. "Why are they shaking hands?"

"Why does anyone shake hands?" Pirep giggled.

Because they've just met, Aon thought. *Or they're friends. Or . . .*

She moved around the memorial to where the mist danced about, creating a new scene. This time, she saw King Isaar flanked by two soldiers whose armor bore the royal crest. The stranger stood across from the king, his fine clothes replaced with a stiff, black robe. At a wave from Isaar, the two soldiers stepped forward. The stranger presented each soldier with a long, flowing robe, which each immediately donned. Isaar watched as the soldiers pulled large hoods over their heads.

Crimson hoods.

"Pirep, what am I watching? Is this the creation of the Crimson Hoods?"

The imp swam around near Aon and gaped up at the shades. "Don't know Crimson Hoods. Only the Architect and his keepers."

"The Architect? Is that the man's name?"

Tali scuttled up onto the island and sat at Aon's feet. "Here, as you see him, he is the Architect. But not for long. Not for long, not for long, not for long."

"Why? What changes that?"

"The Carse, of course. The Carse changes everything."

Aon understood. This wasn't just the creation of the Crimson Hoods. She was witnessing the creation of the Carse itself. It was created by the Architect.

The shades vanished and then reappeared. The Architect presented the hooded robes to Isaar's soldiers again. The Crimson Hoods worked for the Architect . . . who worked for King Isaar.

That's why they shook hands, she realized. *They were making a deal. And turning two royal soldiers into Crimson Hoods was part of that deal.* More than ever before, Aon felt she was genuinely close to some answers.

Before she could interrogate Pirep and Tali further, a rush of wind washed over the island, carrying a distant tune. The song. It was back.

The imps swayed to the music, mesmerized by its eerie melody. Aon hadn't heard it on her last two visits to the Carse. She'd all but forgotten about it. But hearing it again reminded her that someone lived here. And if she wanted real answers—not the riddles of Pirep and Tali—Aon had to find its singer.

Aon waded away from the island, back to the path they'd been following. She raced down the muddy lane until it split into a fork. Her head spun around, trying to pinpoint the singing. But it seemed to be coming from everywhere at once.

"Wait, the Highness!" Pirep called as she and Tali scurried to catch up with Aon. "Wait!"

Aon was about to choose the path to the right when a flash of color down the left path caught her eye. The color stood out in this place that seemed to forbid hue and radiance. She went to the left, squinting into the fog.

And then she saw it, leaning up against a dreadwillow.

A crutch with a wide purple ribbon tied around it.

Chapter Seventeen

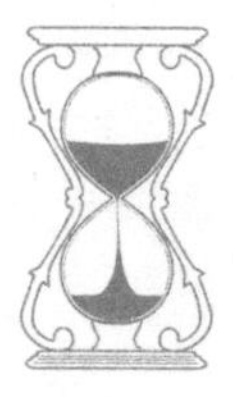

Herrus Tower, the smallest of the Nine Towers, held apartments for the royal servants. All the servants—from Cook to the stable workers—lived in luxury. From any west-facing window, the servants' quarters had an unobstructed view of Ravus Tower, which held the royal apartments.

In the dining hall of Herrus, Jeniah sat on the stony ledge of a window facing Ravus. When she was a girl, she often came to visit the servants here. They told the most wonderful folktales and fed the princess's appetite for stories of magic. Right then, she'd have given anything to have Cook whisk her away with another fanciful tale.

Jeniah stared across the dark courtyard and could just make out the window of her mother's bedchambers. Shadows flitted across the dim light—the healers, no doubt checking on the queen. If the queen woke, the lights would stay on while the healers examined her. If she was still asleep, the lights would vanish as the healers left quickly, in order to avoid disturbing the monarch. Jeniah gripped the window's ledge until her knuckles hurt.

The lights vanished.

Jeniah had never felt more helpless. She didn't care about the Carse anymore. Or the Crimson Hoods. Or what information Aon was gathering in her explorations. None of it mattered. Jeniah wanted to be the princess her mother wanted her to be. The princess everyone expected her to be. At that moment, it seemed far from possible. She couldn't stop thinking about how, with every minute, her mother's life ebbed. If magic existed, Jeniah needed it right that very second.

She heard nearly silent footfalls behind her. The scent of sulfur and lavender assaulted her nose.

"Leave me," Jeniah said, her voice hoarse. But Skonas waited in the doorway, Gerheart atop his shoulder.

"There's not a single person in all of Nine Towers who understands how you feel right now," the tutor said softly. "Except me. Remember, I'm not a royal subject. I'm not like everyone else."

As often as she'd longed to hear real answers from her tutor's lips, these moments—when Skonas wielded truth like a rapier—made Jeniah long for the comfort of a lie. But he was right, and she knew it. Any attempt to tell the maids or footmen the thoughts and feelings that thundered inside her would be met with a smile and a blank stare. She could tell Skonas.

Jeniah studied her tutor's reflection in the window. She suspected a trap. Why this sudden kindness? Perhaps he truly felt sorry for her. Perhaps he really did understand everything that was running through her mind.

"My mother trusts you," Jeniah said. "She thinks you are learned. I'm asking you now, not as Queen Ascendant but as someone who is afraid: What do you know of magic?"

She expected him to laugh. Or maybe just smile gently as all her past tutors had, taking her hand and explaining that magic wasn't real. Instead, he sat next to her on the window ledge and spoke very somberly.

"Magic is misunderstood. Storytellers have had great fun masking its true nature behind spells and incantations and curses. Magic exists, and it is performed every day. It rests in the silence that follows a promise. It thrives in the heart of a selfless act. It stands side by side with courage and love."

Jeniah's heart sank again. "That's poetic," she said, "but it won't help my mother."

"Ah," Skonas said, "so you think you want *magic*, but what you really want is *power*."

"Same thing."

"Not always."

"It doesn't matter. The power to stop my mother from dying doesn't exist."

Skonas nodded sadly. "You're right there. In my life—and I've lived a good number of years—I've seen both magic and power in action. Tell me what you want more: to stop your mother from dying or to be a good queen?"

"Both," Jeniah said. "I want both in equal measure."

"Now tell me: Which do you have the power to affect?"

Jeniah sat quietly. She didn't want to give him the satisfaction of answering.

So Skonas answered for her. "Are you starting to see now? The difference between magic and power?

Being queen is less about wielding power and more about knowing *how* to wield that power."

"I'm stuck, then, aren't I? Because you won't tell me how to wield power. You won't tell me anything. Soon, the people of the Monarchy will gather for my coronation. And the person they're relying on most to defend a thousand years of prosperity will let them down. Because I don't know how to wield power."

Skonas tugged thoughtfully at his beard. "I've taught you three lessons now—" Jeniah scoffed at the notion. "The fourth lesson is still yours to set, but I'll tell you one more thing you should probably know: I can't tell you how to wield power. Oh, sure, you could look back on how all those before you governed and learn from their mistakes. But you'll always encounter problems your ancestors never dreamt about. And then what good will that ancient wisdom get you? In the end, you're better off drawing on what you know and making up your own mind."

I can't tell you how to be queen. I can only tell you how I was queen. Her mother's words came back to Jeniah.

Skonas reached up his billowing sleeve and pulled out a chunk of moldy cheese. He tore off a piece, popped it into his mouth, and said, "I think you want to be a good queen more."

Jeniah looked at him, horrified. "How can you say that?"

"Because you already know that no power can save your mother. She is going to die, and when that happens, all you'll have left is your crown. You will *have* to go on. So you feel guilty that you're not thinking more about your mother."

Skonas leaned in. "It's all right, Your Highness. You're allowed to be scared for yourself. Your mother understands, I promise you."

Something deep within Jeniah shifted. A hundred knots unfurled. A thousand burdens took flight. She'd been wanting—needing—to hear these words but never even knew it.

"It's a good sign," Skonas said, slipping the cheese back up his sleeve. "The fact that you're worrying about your own future while worrying that your mother has none. It shows great promise."

They sat quietly. Jeniah pressed her forehead against the cool glass and peered into the night sky.

"So," Jeniah said, "what's an answer?"

"I'm sorry?"

"You once told me that questions are the lamplight that leads us from darkness. What are answers?"

Skonas took her by the shoulders and gently guided

her a quarter turn to the left. Out the window, she could see the gardens, bright as day. Skonas pointed to the memorial for the past monarchs that burned like a small sun.

"Answers are the pyre that banishes darkness altogether."

Jeniah stared into the distant flame. So, her search for answers had been the right thing after all. Strange, how it brought her no comfort.

Skonas cleared his throat. "Now, about that fourth lesson . . ."

"Your Highness?" Jeniah glanced over her shoulder to see her maid, Sirilla, peeking into the room. She was grateful for the interruption. "I'm sorry to disturb you, Princess," Sirilla continued, "but . . . well, there's a boy at the gates. He's asking to see you. He said he was sent by 'Aon.'"

The princess stiffened. She stood, straightened her dress, and moved across the dining hall. "Take me to him."

"Jeniah."

The princess stopped at her tutor's soft beckoning. When she turned back to him, he wore the same look on his face as he had on their first meeting in the library, when he had told her that the fourth lesson would be imprinted on her soul. This was only the second time she'd seen that very serious look.

"Your mother is dying, and you can't change that," Skonas said. "You'll do best to consider what you *can* change."

Jeniah sighed. She'd grown weary of Skonas's riddles. She allowed Sirilla to usher her from the room. The maid wrapped a warm cloak around the princess's shoulders as they walked away.

A pair of royal guards stepped in line behind Jeniah as she emerged from the towers and walked to the gates. A patchwork of moon and torchlight guided her to where a boy with a long neck shivered in the night air.

The boy stared, bright-eyed, through the bars of the gates, his brown hair pitched this way and that. In his hands, he held a large hourglass. When he caught sight of the princess, the boy broke into a wide grin.

"Do you have a message from Aon?" Jeniah asked.

The boy held up the hourglass, every grain of its sparkling sand resting in the lower chamber. He never stopped smiling, but when he spoke, the princess's blood chilled.

"She didn't come out," he said.

Chapter Eighteen

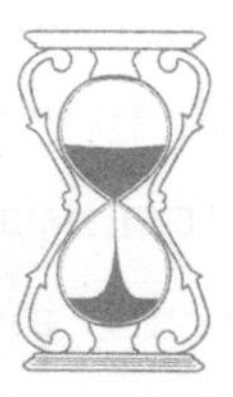

"*WHERE IS HE?*"

Aon hadn't even heard herself scream the question. The rage that set her every limb aflame left her blind and unthinking. She wanted to tear the Carse apart. She wanted to turn every hideous dreadwillow tree from here to Emberfell into kindling. All this time she'd been coming here for answers, hoping they would lead to her father's release. No wonder Jeniah couldn't find Aon's father. He'd been hidden in the one place the princess could never look.

With a war cry, Aon swung the crutch back and forth like a scythe, missing Pirep and Tali by scant inches. The imps cried out and scrambled about, zigzagging as Aon swatted at them.

Aon could barely speak. She wrapped the purple ribbon so tightly around her hand, the purple ribbon tore. With a burst of anger, she struck the oozing earth with the crutch. "He's here! My father is here somewhere. Take me to him."

Pirep hid behind Tali and held her hands over her eyes, as though that would prevent Aon from seeing her. Tali tried to burrow into the ground. "We do not know the He!" Pirep wailed. "We do not know the He!"

Tali, unable to hide herself in the mud, started crying. "We serve the Highness. We guide the Highness. Pity Tali and Pirep. Pity us!"

Aon looked around wildly. If her father was here, then it was likely the Crimson Hoods were as well. And she refused to believe the imps hadn't seen any of them.

Over the sniveling of the imps, the slow, wordless waltz continued.

"Whoever that is singing," Aon said, "take me to them. Take me to them right now."

Pirep and Tali huddled close and whispered back and forth. Then Pirep stepped forward cautiously. "The Highness has much to see and learn in the Carse. Later. Tali and Pirep will take the Highness later."

Aon picked up the crutch and held it over her head as if ready to strike. Pirep ducked and whined. "Now! Now! Tali and Pirep will take the Highness now."

Muttering, the imps waddled down the left path. Aon followed closely behind, keeping them at bay with her father's crutch. The farther they traveled, the louder the singing got. The waltz no longer seemed to come from everywhere; they were clearly headed straight for the source.

Please be with my father, Aon thought. That singing had always brought her comfort in the Carse, and she knew, deep down, that if her father was with the singer, he would be safe.

She suddenly remembered to check the hourglass. Glancing at her waist, she found the bottom bulb had shattered. Probably when she'd been swinging the crutch. She had no idea how long she'd been in the Carse.

Aon held up her hands. Gray skin. Black warts. And her fingers were starting to look like talons.

It didn't matter anymore. She was too close. She couldn't turn back now.

The trail grew more and more narrow. At last, it stopped in front of a wall of briar and thistle that rose up out of the swamp, twisting around itself like wooden lightning. The barbs were as big as Aon.

Monstrous vines reached up and up, threatening to choke the blackened sky itself. The wall stretched as far as she could see in either direction; there was no going around it.

"As the Highness wishes," Pirep said, bowing awkwardly. She and Tali stepped aside to allow Aon to approach.

The girl studied the briar. The points on the thorns glistened like glass. She assumed they were poisonous.

"What I want is behind this wall, yes?" Aon picked up a fallen dreadwillow branch and poked at the briar. The thorns sliced the stick into splinters.

"Everything the Highness wants is there," Tali confirmed.

"Is there a way through?" Aon could hear the singing louder than ever. It was definitely coming from the other side of the briar wall. But she could see no opening, and the thorns would easily impale her if she got too close. "Tell me how—"

But when she looked down to her guides, their mischievous, helpful faces were gone. The imps had inflated to nearly twice their size. They reminded Aon of a cat that had arched its back in preparation for a fight.

"She is not the Highness." Pirep, who had always been the more polite of the pair, had changed her tone sharply. Her bulbous eyes glared murderously at Aon. Aon stumbled. The bravery she'd felt swinging the crutch around drained away as both imps advanced slowly, dangerously.

"She is not the Highness," Tali agreed, baring razor-sharp teeth.

Aon quickly pulled out the royal crest. "You have seen this," she said, trying to sound regal. It didn't work. "You know who I am."

"The heart of the Carse always opens for the Highness," Tali said. "It has always opened for every Highness. *You* are not the Highness."

Aon felt her stomach drop.

"What do you mean it has always opened for every Highness?" she asked, trying to buy time. "No monarch has ever been inside the Carse."

But the imps wouldn't be distracted. With a growl, Pirep lurched forward, snapping with her jaw and biting off the end of the crutch.

"Told you it was for eating," Tali said.

Aon withdrew slowly as the hungry imps bore down. Behind her, she could sense the wicked thorns of the briar wall. She had nowhere to run.

This is the heart of the Carse, she thought. That was what Tali had called it. Not just the center. The *heart*. This was where the Carse kept the misery and woe it collected. And that was what was going to save her now. She knew what it wanted. The Carse wanted the greatest sadness Aon knew. It *needed* her to share the one sorrow she had sworn to never, ever share.

She thought back to that first encounter with Pirep and Tali. She'd told them the story of Jeniah's losing her mother. The only way out now was to tell her own story.

"Once," Aon said, "there was a broken girl who had a secret."

The imps froze. Their eyes gleamed. The creatures, like the Carse, craved sadness. They were about to get a feast.

"For most of her life, she hadn't known she was broken. When she found out, she suddenly had a secret. But the fact that she was broken was *not* the secret. The girl's secret was her mother.

"Everyone knew the girl's mother. She was the happy woman whose glassblowing skills were second to none in all the land. She was the generous woman who cared for the sick and never took a single coin in payment. In many ways, the girl's mother was the heart of their community.

"The girl loved her mother deeply. The mother called her daughter 'rose blossom.' When she taught the girl to blow glass, she would say, 'The hourglass must be perfectly formed, rose blossom.' And even when the girl got it wrong, her mother would give her a hug and say, 'Your next hourglass will be perfect.'

"The girl and her mother lived with the girl's father, a kind, gentle man who was blinded by his own happiness. At least, that was how the mother described him. But she loved her husband despite this. She maybe even loved him because of this. Because happy was something the mother, it seemed, could never really be.

"One day, when the girl was very young, she found her mother in a corner of the kitchen. The mother sat with her back to the wall, tears rolling down her face. The little girl had never seen anyone cry before. The sight lit an infant flame inside her. She couldn't help it; she started crying, too. Mother and daughter held each other and cried.

"'You must never tell anyone,' the mother said when they'd finished. 'This is just for us to share. If we keep this to ourselves, I'll tell you things no one else knows. I'll share with you my greatest secret.'

"And each night, as she tucked the girl into bed,

the mother would teach her daughter secret words. 'There is a language,' she told the girl, 'that was lost a long time ago. There are words that people use, but their meaning has faded. These are words you need to know. My mother taught me, and now I will teach you.'

"That was how the girl came to understand 'sadness.' And 'grief.' And 'dread,' a word used often by everyone but understood by none. Alone in the girl's room, mother and daughter spoke their own private language, forgotten words of sorrow that brought them happiness to share.

"And when the girl was older, the mother fulfilled the promise to share her greatest secret. At the edge of the town where they lived sat a dark copse. A wood so murky it seemed to feed on darkness and woe. The mother took her daughter to see the woods.

"'When I feel sad, and I don't want anyone else to see, I go in there,' the mother said, pointing to the woods. 'You are too young to go in, but when the time is right, I will take you there with me, rose blossom.'

"The young girl agreed to keep the secret. Each night, she dreamt about the day her mother would finally take her into the woods where she could feel less broken.

"This went on for years. The girl watched her

mother return renewed from the darkened copse. This, the mother said, gave her the strength to be happy. It was a strength she dearly needed, in a land where joy was all around. Each time she returned, the mother promised to take the girl inside once she was old enough.

"Late one evening, the mother roused the girl from a deep sleep. The girl, her mind hazy and heavy with dreams, knew immediately her mother had been to the dark copse that night. Usually, her mother returned calmer and with the strength to hide her sadness.

"But not this time. Something was different. The mother held the girl close and ran her fingers through her daughter's hair. The girl was still tired and almost fell asleep as her mother rocked her gently. Her mother's words washed over her like a distant song.

"'Rose blossom,' the mother said, 'I must go away. Far, far from the Carse, from the Monarchy . . . and from you. I *cannot* stay. In many ways, I hope someday you will understand why. In other ways, I pray you never do. There are things I've seen that have changed everything. I know now who I really am and who I can never be.'

"The girl didn't understand. It sounded like a

riddle. As she drifted off to sleep in her mother's arms, she told herself to ask her mother about the answer in the morning.

"But when the little girl woke, her mother was truly gone.

"The girl never saw her mother again. She never found out where her mother had gone. Or why. She knew only that her mother had seen something so terrifying, so horrific, so *unspeakable*, that her only choice was to leave the land that brought everyone so much happiness and never return.

"Not a single person noticed the mother had gone. The girl was helpless as everyone around her—the people of her town, her own father—quietly erased the mother from their lives in the name of being happy. It stung the girl to see how little it took for them to forget this woman they all claimed to love. But the girl would never forget.

"She felt more broken than ever. She asked herself over and over: Why couldn't her mother have taken the girl with her where she went? Why couldn't they have left and been broken together?"

Aon's throat felt raw. Her eyes burned. She suddenly felt very, very tired. More than anything, she didn't want to say another word.

Pirep and Tali lay still, monstrous grins on their faces. They reminded Aon of her father, resting with contentment after a large, satisfying meal. They wouldn't be attacking any time soon. Safe, she sank to the ground and waited for the Carse to respond.

Nearby, a twig snapped. Then another. Then a thousand more snaps crackled, echoing off the trees and filling the air. The great, tangled vines of briar began to move. They coiled and recoiled like a nest of serpents. Aon stepped back as a hole formed in the wall, the briar parting just enough for her to enter. Fingers wrapped around the royal crest in her pocket, she ducked down and passed through.

Behind her, Aon could hear the vines racing back into place. The hole was gone. She was cut off and on her own in the heart of Dreadwillow Carse.

Chapter Nineteen

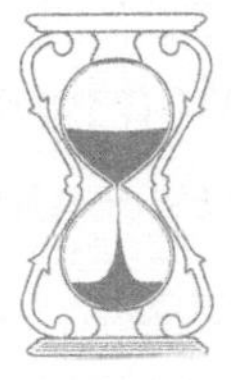

JENIAH HAD BEEN ONLY SIX WHEN HER FATHER, THE KING, died—in a hunting accident on the southern ridge. The days and weeks that followed had overflowed with firsts. It was the first time she'd realized she felt different from the servants who'd cared for her all her life. She hadn't understood why they, too, weren't grieving for her father. It was the first time she'd seen her mother—a woman of such confidence and elegance—shaken to her core. And it was the first time Jeniah had wished with all her heart for magic. Or for anything that could relieve her mother's grief.

In those days, whenever Jeniah found her mother

crying, Queen Sula would immediately wipe her eyes and take the girl to the Grand Hall of Aunx Tower. A lavish room with gilded doorways and great crystal chandeliers, the hall had hosted many a ball in the past. On the walls hung the portraits of every monarch who had ever ruled the land. Her mother had once said that everything Jeniah would ever need to know about their family could be seen in the eyes of those who had come before.

First, mother and daughter would walk through the Grand Hall, and Jeniah would recite the names of the forty monarchs, in order of succession. When this was finished, the queen would reward her daughter by taking her out onto the balcony and reading a story by moonlight.

One night, just a month after her father's death, Jeniah sat on her mother's lap and listened to a story about a sorceress who could commune with rivers, whisper chants that turned into stars, and tame the wiliest dragon by painting its soul with blue she'd plucked from the sky. The stories, which Jeniah even then suspected were meant to make her forget her painful loss, only made her miss her father more. And it had taken the whole month for Jeniah to work up the courage to ask her mother a question.

It took courage because there was an answer that would make Jeniah happy and an answer that would not. "Is magic real?" she asked her mother.

The queen paused. Her gaze became distant, as if she were choosing exactly the right words from a collection etched invisibly on the starry horizon. Then she said, "Love as if it is; live as if it is not."

At the time, Jeniah didn't know what that meant. She only liked the idea that love itself was some kind of magic. That was certainly how she'd felt when her father had been near or when she was on the balcony with her mother, reading stories.

It wasn't until now, as Jeniah followed the dirt road to Emberfell with the village boy leading the way, that she finally understood what her mother had been trying to tell her.

You can't wait around for magic to happen, she thought. Magic wasn't going to recover Aon. Nor was any person, because no one with the power to help knew where she was. Except Jeniah—the person who'd sent Aon into the Carse.

How did Jeniah think she could be queen? Every decision she'd made—sending Aon into the Carse, getting rid of the rubywings—had ended in disaster. And now, by doing the one and only thing she'd ever been forbidden to do, she was about to prove how unfit she was to wear the crown.

As Jeniah followed the long-necked boy toward the Carse, she heard him singing to himself. He seemed unconcerned about his friend's disappearance. Jeniah pulled her cloak tight to her shoulders and sped up until her gait matched the boy's.

"I'm sorry, what was your name again?" Jeniah asked.

The boy huffed with each step. "Laius, Your Majesty."

Jeniah could still hear Skonas, insisting that she could only be called *Your Highness* until she was a real queen. She didn't correct Laius. She wanted someone to call her that just once. After tonight, she might never hear it again.

"Right here, Your Majesty," Laius said, pointing to the gaping maw that led into Dreadwillow Carse. He looked back at Nine Towers. "Are you sure we don't need those guards who offered to come with you?"

It had taken a direct royal order before the guards had agreed not to follow. "No, I'm not sure," Jeniah said, more to herself than to Laius. But she couldn't let anyone find out what she'd done.

Jeniah noticed that Laius kept a safe distance. It was as Aon had described. He wasn't afraid, but he wasn't about to *allow* himself to get close enough to be afraid. It alarmed her that the boy didn't seem at all troubled by Aon's disappearance. He'd sought the princess because he'd been told to, not because he was afraid of what had happened to his friend.

Jeniah couldn't imagine feeling anything but distraught if her mother had vanished. How horrible it would be to disappear and have no one grieve for you. What good was the never-ending bliss of her subjects if it meant they could never truly mourn what they lost? Was real love possible without the fear of loss? Suddenly, the peace and prosperity Jeniah had worried about defending didn't seem so valuable.

The princess held out her lantern and peered into the darkness. She had the strangest feeling the darkness was peering back.

"Are you going in there?" Laius asked, setting the hourglass on the ground. "Are you going to find Aon?"

Jeniah didn't know what to do.

"What would you do if you were me, Laius?" she asked. "What if you had been told that everything you know and love would be destroyed if you set even a foot in that swamp? Would you still do it? To save Aon?"

A flicker of confusion crossed the boy's face. "Are you saying . . . Are you saying you want me to go in there?"

"No," Jeniah replied. "I can't send you. I can't send anybody else."

"You're the Queen Ascendant. You could send the constable."

"I wish it were that easy. If I tell anyone that I sent a girl into the Carse alone . . . well, they wouldn't think very highly of me. And they'd want to know why I did it. No one can know about this."

"Why *did* you send Aon in there?"

Jeniah laughed softly. "I thought I was being clever. I was trying to do something the easy way." She thought about the rubywings. She'd told the farmer to do what was easiest. They'd killed four to save hundreds. Those numbers should have given the princess comfort. And yet they didn't.

"Could you do it, Laius? Could you risk the safety of the Monarchy to save one person, even if you yourself put that person in danger?"

Jeniah searched the boy's face for some sign that he understood what was at stake. But whatever small doubt he'd had earlier was long gone. Now, the boy was grinning happily, just like he was supposed to.

"I would do whatever the monarch told me to do," he said.

Jeniah smiled, and the boy would never understand exactly how sad that smile was.

She closed her eyes. *Only believe what you've seen and heard*, she told herself. *That's what Skonas taught you. You've neither seen nor heard any evidence that the warning is real.*

But you've heard *the warning*, she answered herself. *Therefore, it must be believed.*

It could be wrong. It's just *a warning. There's no magic. You can't destroy the Monarchy by stepping over that border. You've neither seen nor heard* a good reason *for staying out of the Carse.*

Before she lost her nerve, Jeniah pulled her cloak tight around her shoulders and walked toward the Carse.

"Wait!"

Jeniah gasped, startled. "What?"

Laius picked up the hourglass. "Aon always had me turn the hourglass, one turn for every hour she spent in there. I think it was important. Should I turn the glass for you?"

Jeniah shook her head. "Go home, Laius. You've served me well. Go home and sleep. If I haven't returned with Aon by the morning, you can tell the constable." Without waiting for the boy to respond, she stepped into the Carse and disappeared from sight.

Nothing happened. The earth didn't open and swallow her. Fire didn't rain down and incinerate the land. *It was a lie*, Jeniah thought. *The Monarchy didn't fall.* Feeling more confident, she continued onward.

The landscape seemed to bleed shadows. Jeniah could barely see an arm's length ahead. She stepped softly and listened, hoping to get some idea of where to go. But the swamp was dead silent. She hadn't expected that. She'd thought she'd hear insects chirping or the rustling of branches on a breeze. At the very least, she thought she'd hear the burbling of the mire that Aon had described in her letter. But she could barely make out her own staggered breathing as she hiked across the treacherous terrain.

"Aon?" she called, partly to find her friend, partly just to hear *something*.

Silence ate her voice.

"It's Jeniah!" She shouted louder. This time, she could hear her name echo faintly in the distance, bouncing off trees and rocks.

A gust of wind blew out her lantern. Jeniah knelt and raced to relight the wick. When she did, the lantern's soft glow reflected off tendrils of thick mist that rose up from the ground all around.

The mist swirled at Jeniah's feet. It billowed into a blanket that pulsed with a faint gray light. Just past the mist, she could barely see the outline of someone walking across the bog toward her. The whirling fog slowed and slowed as the other person emerged into the light from the princess's lantern.

"Hello, Jeniah," Aon said with a smile.

Chapter Twenty

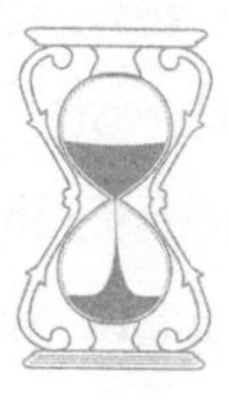

SILENCE ALL AROUND HER, AON STOOD ALONE IN THE CLEARING beyond the wall of briar. It didn't look much different from the rest of the Carse.

The ground was more solid. It was slightly easier to see the starry night sky through the roof of tree branches. The fog was thinner. The stench of sulfur still hung in the air, but with a touch of something pleasant underneath. Lilacs, maybe? Lavender? But otherwise, she didn't notice anything that required a wall of briar to keep people out. The Carse within the briar seemed very much the same as the Carse outside.

Except the trees. The dreadwillows here were sparse and spread out. They were also much smaller than the mammoth ones that crowded the swamp's outer rim. They weren't quite saplings, but their branches weren't yet laden with the festering black moss that covered the full-grown trees beyond the walled-up grove.

They're younger, Aon thought. But that didn't make sense. Surely the trees at the center of the Carse should be the oldest.

Aon scratched her arms. The gray, warty flesh had crawled up to her shoulders. She could feel it slowly inching across her back. *You won't win*, she silently promised the Carse.

The singing was much closer now. The mournful dirge vibrated in her ears. Whenever she'd heard the song before, it brought relief and calm. Now, hearing it so clearly and so near, she could hardly contain her excitement.

"Hello?" she called out. "Who's there?"

No response. The song continued without pause.

"I can hear you singing. Please, I want to talk to you."

Aon ventured farther into the clearing. It didn't seem that far across. She wasn't sure why she couldn't see the singer. Maybe there really were ghosts in the Carse. *Or maybe the trees are singing*, she thought with a laugh.

With every step, she felt the heaviness of the Carse return until it sat like a stone in her chest. The itch spread. Weary, she leaned against a dreadwillow to rest.

The tree moved.

It was ever so slight, but it clearly shifted beneath her hand. Startled, Aon stepped back. The tree's bark rippled across the slender trunk, sliding and rearranging itself. If she'd looked away, she would have missed it. But the dreadwillow had definitely moved.

"They like to be touched."

Aon whirled around to face the gentle voice behind her. The woman who stood just an arm's length away looked down on the girl with warm, familiar eyes. Her round face beamed. Though not a queen, she had a regal authority both wise and welcoming.

"Mother."

For one brief, impossible moment, the Carse's invisible talons—those that clutched Aon's insides—withered as happiness filled Aon completely. She was about to throw herself into her mother's arms, when the woman held her off by raising a hand.

"I'm not your mother, Aon," the woman said. "I'm a shade, like almost everything else you've seen in the Carse. I'm the piece she left behind."

"Left behind?" Aon thought about her first trip into the Carse for the princess. When she'd emerged, she'd felt like she'd left with less of herself. "Did she leave it on purpose?"

"No. But if she knew, I think she'd approve."

Aon's hope and joy rushed away like a flood from a broken dam. If possible, she felt even emptier than when she'd first entered the Carse. "This is cruel," she said.

The shade nodded. "I know. I'm sorry."

Aon squinted at the woman. "You're not like the other shades. I can see through them. But you look . . . real. And you can talk to me."

"The other shades you've seen are very old. I haven't been here as long. Over time, I'll be as they are. I'll start to fade away, my words will be unheard, and I'll relive a single event over and over and over until I'm nothing more than mist off the bogs."

Aon recalled how the shades of King Isaar had repeated their actions: watching the siege of the castle from the balcony, shaking hands with the Architect. "Why does that happen?"

The Mother-shade turned and walked to a nearby dreadwillow. "The pieces people leave behind relive important events. Events that changed the person forever. For me, that was right in this spot. With this tree."

The Mother-shade reached out. Its hand shimmered as it passed through the lowest branch of the dreadwillow. The tree shuddered. The earth at its base pushed up and out, as if a mole were burrowing below. The dreadwillow's roots pulled the tree away just far enough to be out of the shade's reach.

"I thought you said they like to be touched," Aon said.

The Mother-shade smiled. "Not by shades. By humans, yes. It makes them feel connected. Try it. Don't be afraid."

Aon approached the tree and gently placed both palms on its trunk. The branches overhead trembled. The bark swam under her hands, tickling slightly. But the tree didn't retreat as it had when the shade touched it.

"This is why you left, isn't it?" Aon asked. "Something happened here. An event you'll relive over and over."

The Mother-shade couldn't take its eyes off the

tree. It seemed distant and distracted. "Did she leave? It would have happened long after your mother left me behind here. It was probably for the best."

"How can you say that?" Aon said, anger rising. "It hurt when she left. She went knowing I could never show my pain to anyone who would understand."

"She left," the Mother-shade said, turning back slowly, "knowing you would one day come here for answers. I promise it wasn't easy for your mother to leave. Trust that, Aon. It meant so much, having someone to share her sorrow. And it hurt so deeply, knowing the burden you'd bear with or without her. Have you ever wondered why you feel sadness when no one else can? Why the same was true for your mother?"

Aon, who still had her hands pressed to the tree, felt it lean into her touch. "I've wondered that every day of my life."

The Mother-shade knelt down, eye to eye with the girl. "It wasn't just the two of you. Every woman in your family has felt the same thing. Most chose to ignore it. They didn't like being different, so they pretended to be happy like everyone else. Others came to the Carse. If you search hard enough, you'll find their shades roaming the groves as well. Although sometimes they stayed too long and paid the price."

She means Pirep and Tali, Aon thought. So the imps really were her distant relatives. They weren't just a fable.

The Mother-shade sighed. "And a few—a very small number—did what your mother did and left the Monarchy. But not before they'd made it here, to the heart of the Carse."

"But what did they see?" Aon asked. "What did you learn that was so terrible, it made you leave me?"

For the first time, the Mother-shade seemed unable to speak. It stared off into space as if the darkness held the words it so desperately needed. "I want you to think about your mother, Aon. Really think about her. She told you many secrets. But she didn't tell you everything. She had one secret she couldn't explain. Because she didn't understand it herself.

"The sadness that travels through our family's women affects everyone differently. Your mother . . . I . . . felt it more deeply. It was more than just sorrow. It took control of me. Of all the lost, secret words I knew, there were none for what was happening inside me. There were days—oh, those awful days—when it felt like drowning and choking and falling all at once. You must remember times when I acted . . . strangely."

At first, Aon thought the shade was lying. She

remembered her mother just fine. A kind woman. A gentle woman. Loved and admired by all, none more than by Aon and her father.

But.

When Aon pressed back through her memories . . . There were times when her mother remained in bed all day. Aon's father had blamed the flu. But Aon could remember hearing her mother crying softly behind the bedroom door. Yes, there were days when the sadness seemed stronger. When Mother couldn't care for herself. Or Father. Or Aon.

How could I have known? Aon wondered. *I should have helped her. I should have—*

The Mother-shade smiled. "You're not to blame, Aon. Don't ever think that. Your mother left because of what she saw here in the heart of the Carse. Her despair kept her from understanding she could take you, too."

Aon pushed the back of her hand across her cheeks, fending off the unwanted tears. There was much, it seemed, that she didn't understand about how deep her mother's sadness ran. She couldn't imagine that kind of sorrow, but she could see it was real. So she knew why her mother had left her behind. One razor-edged question remained unanswered.

"Tell me. What did she see? What made her want to leave the Monarchy?"

The dreadwillow shifted under her hands again. Aon looked up to find the trunk of the tree had turned nearly all the way around. She was now staring into three misshapen knotholes in the center of the trunk. Two of the knotholes, side by side, narrowed as she watched. The third, just below the two, curved slightly with its ends pointing upward. Almost like a smile. In all, it looked just like . . .

A face.

Gasping, Aon stepped back. She looked around quickly and discovered that all the dreadwillows had turned toward her. All, to some degree or another, had faces. Some were made from knotholes, others from darker shades of bark. Every single one was twisted with agony.

Aon stumbled. When she backed into a dreadwillow, she spun around. It was very young. Branches had only just started to sprout from the top of the trunk. But the branches weren't the same dark gray color as the bark at the roots of the tree. They were paler. Pinkish beige.

They looked like flesh.

"The trees are people," Aon said, horrified. "People who wandered into the Carse . . ."

The Mother-shade appeared at her side. "No one enters the Carse of their own will. You know that."

"Then . . . these are my ancestors? The ones who came to the Carse for relief?"

"You've met Pirep and Tali," the Mother-shade said. "You know what happened to those unlucky few."

"Who are they, then?" Aon pulled her hand across the face of the tree before her, as though brushing someone's cheek. The tree shuddered, and Aon understood it was grateful for her touch.

Aon once again heard the dirge. The sad, haunting waltz had never stopped, but its presence had faded while she spoke with the shade. Aon held out her lantern, searching for the source. The Mother-shade had vanished. Aon was about to call out for it when, just ahead, she spotted two silhouettes kneeling at the base of a dreadwillow.

"You!" she cried out, racing across the clearing. But once she got close enough for her light to illuminate the pair, she froze in place.

The duo, their faces hidden by crimson hoods, tended to the tree before them. One pulled weeds from near the dreadwillow's roots while the other poured murky water from a rusty pail onto the base of the tree.

Her eyes ran up the dreadwillow's trunk. Sure enough, the bark higher up was mottled. The color faded from dark gray to pinkish beige. This dreadwillow was so young, it hadn't sprouted any branches at all. On one side of the trunk, an arm—still very human—hung limply. On the other side, the arm had begun turning into a branch, fingers replaced with twigs, skin replaced with wood. And in the center of the trunk, a face made of bark and flesh stared back, a look of horror permanently etched across its features.

It was the face of Aon's father.

Chapter Twenty-one

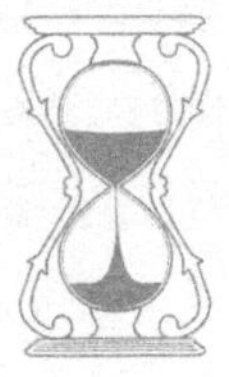

JENIAH'S FIRST INSTINCT HAD BEEN TO GRAB AON'S HAND, TURN, and run. They couldn't have been more than twenty feet from the entrance of the Carse. They could have been out in a second and sorted out any problems once they were safely on the road to Emberfell.

But no. No, it was too easy.

"Laius did as you instructed," the princess said cautiously. "The time ran out on his hourglass, so he came to get me. He said you told him I'd know what to do. All I knew to do was come in here looking for you. And here you are."

"I'm glad you're here, Jeniah," Aon said. "It's so brave of you to come rescue me."

The girl reached out, but Jeniah backed away.

"You're not Aon," the princess said. "She never could bring herself to call me Jeniah."

Jeniah tried to bat Aon's hand away, but her fingers passed through. The princess yelped in pain. Frost crystals formed on her fingertips, and stinging cold numbed her hand.

"You're a shade," Jeniah said. "She told me about you."

The Aon-shade looked Jeniah up and down curiously, as if it had never seen a human before. "It's dangerous for a princess to travel without a guard escort."

"I have nothing to fear from my subjects," Jeniah replied, chin held high.

"True," the Aon-shade said. "And yet, the royal family keeps an army of guards. Every town has a constable. Prisons, unused for centuries, remain standing. Have you ever wondered why? What's the point of having soldiers and prisons in a land that knows nothing but peace?"

Jeniah wasn't about to admit it, but she *hadn't* ever wondered why. She'd always just accepted these facts. Now, the shade's words made her see how foolish she had been never to question them.

"I'm sure you'll tell me," Jeniah said to the shade.

The Aon-shade leaned in close and whispered, "They protect the Monarchy from you."

Jeniah flinched. Obviously, the shade was trying to upset her, confuse her. That was it. The shade would say anything to trick her.

But then she thought about everything Aon had told her about the war King Isaar had stopped. Ice pinched at her neck. "Somehow, my coming here starts a war. That's what the warning means."

The Aon-shade flashed a sly grin. "No, not exactly. But you're on the right track. You're expected, you know. Come."

The shade turned and walked deeper into the bog. Jeniah followed.

"Did you think I'd be fooled?" Jeniah asked. "You don't act anything like Aon. There's a coldness to your eyes."

"Sometimes shades are who they seem," the Aon-shade replied. "Other times, they serve as vessels."

Vessels? Then Jeniah realized. Vessels for the Carse. That was who—what—was speaking to her now.

"Why do you look like her?" Jeniah asked.

"I'm a bit of Aon that she left behind. Everyone who enters the Carse leaves a part behind."

"*What* part?"

"Everyone hides a part of who they really are from the rest of the world," the Aon-shade said. "But the part people leave behind here is something that *needs* to be seen by others."

"It will happen to me, too, I suppose," Jeniah mused. "I'll leave part of me behind when I leave, won't I?"

The Aon-shade smirked. "Oh, we're counting on it."

Of course they were, whoever *they* were. The shade had said Jeniah was expected. Why? How could anyone have known she'd come here?

The part people leave behind here is something that needs *to be seen by others.* Jeniah puzzled over this. If this was true, it meant she, too, would leave part of herself behind. What, she wondered, would she need others to see?

The Aon-shade squinted back at the princess. "Weren't you told to stay out?"

"I was told the Monarchy would fall if I entered," Jeniah said. "But that didn't happen."

"Didn't it?" the shade challenged. "You're not in the Monarchy anymore, remember? You don't know what's happened outside the Carse. For all you know, you've shattered the happiness that Mad King Isaar worked so hard to give his people. When you step outside the Carse, you could find your land in ruins."

"Is that what's happening?"

The Aon-shade turned away. "I think I'll leave that for a surprise."

The dirt path they followed curved sharply. By now, Jeniah's eyes had grown accustomed to the dim light. She could see the path lined with dreadwillow trees on either side, forming a corridor, their branches arching overhead like a canopy made from a murder of ravens.

"Where are you taking me?" Jeniah asked.

"Exactly where you need to go," the Aon-shade said, "to see exactly what you need to see."

As they walked between the rows of dreadwillows, a shimmer of gray light to the left drew Jeniah's gaze. Between two trees, a glowing mist rose up out of the bog. With a faint *click*, the mist formed another shade, this one faded and pale.

"King Isaar!" Jeniah said. The shade nodded solemnly in her direction. Had it heard her?

Another flash, another *click.* A new shade, wan and insubstantial, appeared between the trees to the right. This one looked like Isaar's daughter and heir, Queen Luris.

Jeniah walked on. A sound like steady rain on a tin roof surrounded her. More and more lights quivered into existence between the trees, joining with the fog to make a legion of shades.

"Queen Herrus . . . Queen Lithe . . . King Ravus . . ." Jeniah ticked off each name as the shades winked into view. It was like being back in the Grand Hall, surrounded by the portraits of all the monarchs. And while these shades stood perfectly still like those paintings, their mouths moved, forming unheard words. As Jeniah passed, they followed her with their eyes.

"They're trying to speak. Do you know what they're saying?"

"Yes." The Aon-shade said no more.

Jeniah slowed down and counted softly to herself. Forty. All forty of the land's previous monarchs were here, standing now as echoes between the dreadwillows. Even her grandmother, the least faded of all the shades. If she listened closely, Jeniah thought she could almost make out what her grandmother was saying . . .

"Wait," Jeniah said. "Why are they here?"

The Aon-shade turned, a glint in its eye as if it had been waiting for this question. "You already know the answer to that, Jeniah. You tried to dismiss it the minute you saw Isaar, but you know . . ."

There was only one reason they could all possibly be here. As hard as she'd been searching for the truth, she hadn't been prepared for this.

"They're here," she said softly, "because they each left a piece of themselves behind. Every monarch has been to the Carse."

Every monarch has defied the warning.

And the Monarchy had never fallen. So what was the point of the warning? Why pass it on, generation after generation, if it clearly wasn't true? All this time, Jeniah had been terrified of bringing some unknown wrath down upon her people, destroying their happiness, and laying waste to all. But it was a lie.

"Jeniah!"

Her head spun, searching for the familiar voice. There, at the end of the path, stood Jeniah's mother. She could barely make the queen out in the fog, but it was clearly her.

"Jeniah! Come here at once."

Jeniah moved around the Aon-shade and stumbled through the muck toward Queen Sula. Breathless, she fell to her knees at her mother's feet.

"Mother," Jeniah said, panting, "you shouldn't be here. You're not well."

"I couldn't trust you," the queen said, seething. Jeniah had never heard this tone from her mother, a woman whose strongest rebuke was gentle if firm. "You were told to stay out of the Carse. Clearly, you're not ready to be monarch."

Jeniah sobbed. It had all been a test. Just to see if she was ready. And she'd failed.

"I'm sorry, Mother. Please, we have to get you back to Nine Towers before—"

She felt something tickle her wrist. Then her ankle. Alarmed, she looked down and found vines of mirebramble slithering out of the ground and wrapping themselves around her arms and legs. She tried to jump up, but the vines held tight, pulling her back down.

"Mother, help!" the princess cried, struggling against the bramble.

The queen scowled. "This isn't how a monarch behaves."

Jeniah gasped and sputtered as the mirebramble snaked around her neck and pulled her face closer and closer to a nearby pond of bubbling muck.

Jeniah looked up at her mother. When she stared

hard enough, she realized she could *just barely* see through her mother's face. The queen was just another trick of the Carse. Something else she couldn't believe, even though she'd seen and heard it. Betrayed and beaten, Jeniah was finally ready to give up.

"You *know* what to do, Jeniah."

The voice of the Aon-shade whispered softly behind her. Out of the corner of her eye, Jeniah saw the shade wink out of existence.

She *did* know what to do. She relaxed. She exhaled slowly and forced herself to stop struggling. The mirebramble pulled her face underwater . . . and then released her.

Jeniah slowly lifted her head as the mirebramble retreated. She remained where she was until the vines moved far away, and then she looked up at the Queen-shade. It was no longer scowling. If anything, it looked guilty that it had tricked her. Somewhere behind her, Jeniah heard a voice. Singing. The princess slowly got to her feet, never taking her eyes off her mother.

That's what I want. I need to find whoever is singing, Jeniah thought.

As if it could hear her, the Queen-shade nodded once and disappeared into the fog.

Jeniah waited for the last of the limp mirebramble

to slink away, picked up her lantern, and plunged back into the Carse. The singing wended its way between the trees ahead. Determined, the princess marched straight toward it.

All Jeniah wanted now was to find Aon and get out. She resolved to forget all of this once she was back in Nine Towers. The torturous silence. The deathless shades. And the knowledge that even her mother—the woman who had warned her away from the black bog every single day of Jeniah's life—had been in the Carse.

Chapter Twenty-two

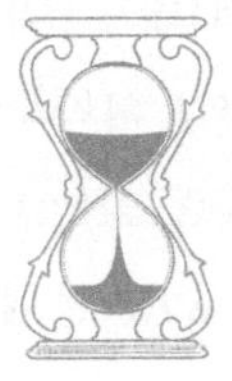

AON HAD NO IDEA HOW LONG SHE'D BEEN KNEELING IN THE MUD. Finding her father planted in the ground and slowly becoming a dreadwillow tree had drained the last bit of energy from her body. She barely remembered falling to her knees. She vaguely recalled crying and crying and crying until she could stand it no longer. After that, she had sat in the mud, feeling hollow and abandoned.

She'd wanted to know why her mother left. And the answer had stolen her faith in the Monarchy, her queen, and everything she'd held dear.

Aon pressed her hands deep into the mud, letting

the earth slowly swallow them. They were claws now, really. Crooked and scaly. She could feel her back hunch forward. She was becoming an imp, like Pirep and Tali. And she didn't care.

The Crimson Hoods paid her no notice. After they'd tended to her father, they moved on to another dreadwillow. They never spoke, but they treated each tree with gentleness. A strange compassion, given that it was the Hoods who'd done this to the people within the trees. And through it all, the singing never stopped. Aon had come to hate the tune. It could no longer ease her misery. But then, she'd never felt a pain like this before. A pain so blinding, so sharp, she'd had to go numb just to push it away. The reprieve was only temporary.

Aon had no reason to return to Emberfell, now that she knew she'd never see her father again. Now that she knew what had driven her mother off. She had no reason to find Jeniah, knowing that the Hoods *did* work for the Monarchy. She didn't know if Jeniah knew the truth, but she knew she could never trust another monarch again.

This won't end, she thought. *This pain will never, ever stop. I know that.*

"I'm sure it feels that way now. But it won't always."

The voice, deep and rumbling, came at the precise moment the singing stopped. Aon didn't even look up. Out of the corner of her eye, she saw someone approach. She could make out only the hem of a stiff, black robe and furry bare toes peeking out from under.

"Who are you?" Aon asked, hoarse from crying. She looked up to see a figure in a robe much like the Crimson Hoods', only this person's face was hidden under a black hood. The voice and the toes suggested a man.

"Do you like the song?" the man in the hood asked. "The dreadwillow trees do. They find it soothing. Of course, I'm sure they prefer your touch. But there are many trees in the Carse—so very many—and I doubt you have time to bring relief to them all." He pointed to her neck, where gray scales were creeping up toward her face. "No. You don't have that much time."

"Who are you?" Aon asked again.

"I go by many names. Here, now, it's probably best that you think of me as the Chorister of Dreadwillow Carse. For that's what I do here. I sing to the trees. I ease their suffering."

"The trees are suffering?" Aon's heart beat so fiercely, she could feel it in her ears. It was hard enough to see her father's face melded into the trunk of a tree, but she couldn't stand to think he was also suffering.

"Not all of them," the Chorister said. "The oldest, the ones outside the briar wall, they're just trees now. They stopped being people a long time ago. Humans weren't meant to endure endless misery. Eventually, a dreadwillow sheds the last of its humanity to put a stop to the pain. But these inside the heart of the Carse will spend many more years feeding on what they need most."

"You're *making* them suffer!" Aon shouted.

"They suffer because it's what a dreadwillow knows. Ever seen a moth dance around a flame? They're drawn to the fire, even though that attraction will eventually consume them. The dreadwillows live on misery, despair, melancholy. Their roots reach deep into the earth, spreading across the Monarchy. To survive, the trees leech these feelings from all who live here. But sadness is their flame, and once they attain it, the pain is unimaginable. So I sing."

He demonstrated. That soft, mournful tune filled the air. As it did, the nearby dreadwillows shifted, their branches relaxing.

Aon stared down. The roots of these trees were

barely underground. But these were the newest dreadwillows—the people most recently taken by the Crimson Hoods. The older trees would surely have roots that dug much deeper if they spread all across the Monarchy.

"That's why everyone is happy," Aon said. "That's what King Isaar did."

The Chorister stopped singing. "Isaar had just emerged victorious in the bloodiest war the Monarchy had ever seen. He was eager to ease the suffering of his people, and so the Carse was made. A place to keep all the Monarchy's woes. Now everyone lives a prosperous life filled with joy."

"I don't!" Aon spat, choking on her own words. "You drove my mother off. And then you took my father. Your dreadwillows don't feed on *my* sadness. I'm left to *feel* it."

The man in the hood folded his hands at his waist. "The Carse has never affected the women in your family. You, your mother, Pirep, Tali . . . It goes back a thousand years, back to a single woman who felt a sorrow so strong, it would pass to every generation in her family."

Aon had never heard of this woman. "Why? Why was she so sad?"

For the first time, the Chorister hesitated. When he spoke, pain colored each word. "She loved her husband very much. And she lost him when he made a foolish deal with the king. She watched herself age while her husband remained untouched by time because of the terms of that bargain. That ache passed from daughter to daughter to daughter. Even now, it's felt by those who don't truly understand it."

Aon's mouth went dry. For the first time, she *did* understand. She'd seen the shade of the man who'd made a deal with Isaar. The imps had called him the Architect. If the woman the Chorister was describing had been the Architect's wife, and the wife's sorrow at losing her husband had afflicted all the women descended from her, then that meant the Architect was Aon's—

"What would you say if I told you," the Chorister said quickly, his distant manner changing abruptly, "that it was possible for your father to leave here and return to his life in Emberfell?"

Aon forgot about the Architect. Her chest swelled. She brushed the hair from her eyes and fought to stand. "Yes. Yes, please." The words tumbled out. "You don't know what it's been like. No one in Emberfell understands what it means to lose someone. If their father dies or their mother is taken by the Crimson Hoods, their lives go on. It's like . . . It's like they're happy, but they can't feel everything that love brings. Or the pain that comes from losing love. I do. I feel it. I'm broken. I'm not like them. I miss my father. I need him."

The Chorister raised a finger of warning. "Bear in mind: the Carse must have its due. In exchange for your father, someone must take his place. Someone that you choose."

A slight breeze whistled mournfully through the dreadwillow branches. Aon found herself struggling to speak. "Someone *I* choose?"

"You. Say the word. Choose someone, anyone. Your father will be returned, and the person you name will take his place."

Aon's mind swam at the possibilities. Whom would she choose? *How* could she choose? Mrs. Crandwyn. Laius. Her vision filled with the faces of everyone she'd ever known in Emberfell. She pictured them planted in the black earth, bark forming on their skin, their limbs becoming crooked branches. Everyone was someone else's brother or father or sister or mother. Could she really do that to another person?

But they're not like me, Aon thought. If she chose

Mrs. Grandwyn, her husband and family wouldn't care. Their lives would go on. They had no choice. The Carse would silently sap the pain of losing a family member, leaving them with only the bliss of having known them. Whom would it really hurt to choose someone, *anyone*?

"They should decide," Aon said, pointing to the Crimson Hoods. "They always choose. Why does it have to be me?"

"It's an exchange, my dear," the Chorister said. "That's how it works. That is how it has always worked. The Carse gives you something; you give the Carse something. That is how it will always work. To free your father, you must choose his successor."

"Does it have to be someone I know? Could I choose a stranger from another town?"

The Chorister considered. "You could. But suppose for a moment that you're not alone. Suppose another girl, somewhere in the Monarchy, can also feel loss, and the stranger who takes your father's place is someone she loves. What's to stop her from striking a similar bargain by trading her loved one for someone randomly chosen? What's to stop that random choice from being your friends, your neighbors . . . or your father again?"

Aon reached out and wrapped her fingers around the end of the branch that had once been her father's arm. Only two fingers remained at the end. The rest were now twigs. "Then I choose myself. I'll take his place."

The Chorister tsked. "Very admirable, but not possible, I'm afraid."

Aon frowned. "Why not? You didn't say there were conditions. The Carse gives; I give. That's what you said. Well, I'm giving myself."

"Exchanges aren't just in goods and services. This exchange is also an exchange of knowledge. An understanding of what the exchange truly means. Your father would learn nothing. He'll leave here and never give another thought to you, the daughter who sacrificed everything for him. He'll return to Emberfell and start life anew."

It hurt to hear that. But Aon knew it was true.

"Something must be learned from the exchange. If you become one with the Carse, you don't learn. It must be someone else. Now . . ." The Chorister paused and leaned in. "Can you do it?"

But Aon didn't have an answer. "I don't know."

The Chorister chuckled softly. "That's a very good answer. I hope you'll remember it."

"Remember it? Why?"

"You're very lucky. You don't *have* to make that choice. Maybe, someday, you'll be grateful to understand that. I hope you can sympathize with someone who *must* make that choice."

Aon swallowed. "Who's that?"

The Chorister pointed to the wall of briar. "The only person in all the Monarchy who can change things."

At that moment, the wall of briar shuddered. The terrible vines snapped and cracked as they ambled aside, creating an opening just as they had done for Aon. The Chorister held out his arms in welcome as a tall, lean silhouette ducked down to pass through the briar's opening and enter the clearing.

"Princess Jeniah," the Chorister called out. "I believe you're right on time."

Chapter Twenty-three

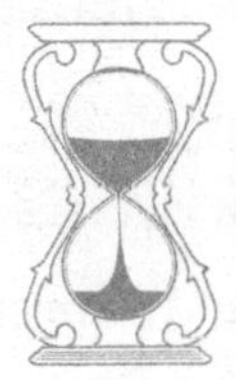

As Jeniah stepped into the heart of the Carse, she let her hand slide into her robe and felt the dagger she'd hidden there. It was clear she couldn't trust anything here. She saw Aon near a sickly-looking dreadwillow—unless it was just another shade. Not far from Aon, a hooded figure with arms outstretched beckoned her closer.

"I wasn't sure you would make it," the man in the robe intoned. "But you've had much on your mind, haven't you?"

Jeniah ignored the man and walked toward Aon. The girl moved a step closer to the tree and wouldn't meet the princess's gaze. It was only when she'd nearly reached Aon that Jeniah noticed the dreadwillow had a human arm and face blistered with bark. Then she looked more closely at Aon. The girl's skin had gone gray, and her hands were now claws.

"What's happened?" Jeniah asked Aon. But the girl remained silent.

Two more figures, wearing the crimson hoods that Aon had once described, seemed to float across the foggy ground until they came to a stop behind the man who had greeted Jeniah. "So, they're real," the princess said. "I should have guessed they were from the Carse. That's why my mother said they were a myth."

"Now, Your Highness," the black-hooded man said with a wag of his finger, "I think we're past pretending that your mother didn't know about the Hoods."

Jeniah regarded the hooded figure coolly. "Tell me your name."

"I go by many names," the man said. "Once, I was known as a healer. Later in my life, I was called a mystagogue. At one point, I was known as—"

"The Architect." Aon, who had said nothing since Jeniah's arrival, spoke softly now. Her face was a mask of bewilderment and bottled rage.

The hooded man paused and then gave a curt nod. "Indeed. You, Princess, may call me the Chorister."

But Jeniah turned her back on him. He was playing games, and she would have none of it.

"Aon, come with me. We're going to leave here—"

"Just tell me one thing . . ." Aon's cheeks flushed. "Did you know? Did you know what was going on here? Did you know my father was being turned into a dreadwillow?" She draped herself against the nearby tree; its human arm fluttered as if wanting to hold and console her.

"You know I didn't," Jeniah said, reaching out her hand. But Aon wouldn't take it. "I would never have sent you in here if I'd known about any of this. But I'm starting to understand more about—"

"Understand?" the Chorister scoffed. "You know nothing of what the Monarchy once was. You don't know the horrors of the war that Isaar brought to an end. When the smoke had cleared, when the battlefields had been emptied, the people demanded peace. Isaar was a good man. He wanted nothing more than to give his people the peace they so deserved.

"So he struck a pact. His people would be happy. His people would be prosperous. They would never again know sorrow or heartache. But these feelings couldn't just be banished. They needed to be taken. Silently, painlessly gathered up."

Jeniah glanced behind Aon at the girl's father. "The dreadwillows."

"With roots that spread throughout the Monarchy. They did exactly as Isaar wanted. Secretly touching the heart of every woman, man, and child and carving out the sadness. Leeching it into the Carse, like drawing poison from a wound."

"So," Jeniah said cautiously, "the dreadwillows are like a cure. Melancholy is a sickness, and the Carse keeps the Monarchy from getting sick by keeping everyone happy."

"Perhaps," the Chorister said. "Although, happiness achieved at the expense of others is its own special brand of poison."

Before Jeniah could question what he meant, the horrible truth dawned. Her mother's face, little more than a withered husk, appeared in her mind. She turned away from the Chorister. But the Chorister wasn't about to let the princess forget his meaning.

"Some monarchs live longer than others," he continued. "They find ways of living with the guilt. They convince themselves that the peace and prosperity enjoyed by thousands is well worth the suffering of just four souls a year. But other monarchs, the ones who let their decision eat them alive from inside . . . They die far too young. Wouldn't you agree, Your Highness?"

Jeniah closed her eyes and tried to summon a different picture of her mother. She wanted to remember how the queen looked a year ago when she was still full of life and energy. But now all she could see was how tightly Queen Sula's once beautiful, dark skin pulled on her thinning, sickly face. A sickness, it seemed, the queen had brought on herself.

"That's why King Isaar ordered the attack on his own castle," Aon said. "He couldn't live with the guilt, once he saw the pain it caused the people who were chosen to become dreadwillows."

"You're saying *you* created the Carse," Jeniah said to the Chorister. "You're saying Isaar ordered you—"

"Ordered?" The Chorister chuckled. "Not exactly. He struck a deal, remember?"

"That would make you more than a thousand years old."

The Chorister drew in a deep, loud breath. "Bargains can be very powerful and should never be made lightly." Was that . . . *regret* in his voice? Had a thousand years as the bog's keeper tempered the Chorister's feelings on Isaar's bargain?

All this talk of bargains. Jeniah felt sick. If this was the magic she'd sought all her life, she wanted no part of it. But, like it or not, she was tied to this magic. Of that, she was certain.

"I understand," the Chorister said, "that you're learning how to be queen. Have you come to any conclusions yet?"

Jeniah leveled an angry glare at the man. "I've learned more about how not to be a queen than how to actually be one."

The Chorister seemed impressed. "Oooh, now that was an interesting answer. Very well. I'll tell you. There is only one thing you need to know in order to be queen. It has nothing to do with etiquette or diplomacy. You need only know the price of happiness in your Monarchy.

"Your people will thrive and prosper. They will never need. Your name will be hallowed. In exchange . . ." The Chorister paused to run his hand across the bark that framed Aon's father's face. "In exchange, you consent that a single person each season will bear the ills meant for all. The Crimson Hoods will continue to harvest willing volunteers to become dreadwillows. These four people will suffer unimaginable pain. The Carse will flourish, each dark bud and bloom growing healthier with every unshed tear.

"But . . . thousands and thousands will continue to live in bliss. And you, Your Highness, you will be *beloved*. You will be the greatest monarch who ever lived."

"They're only 'willing volunteers' because they've been lied to," Aon pointed out.

"The Monarchy *cannot* know unhappiness," the Chorister said. "Tell any commoner the truth. They'll still go willingly because they can't comprehend how a dreadwillow suffers."

"This is what the warning means, isn't it?" Jeniah asked. "I wasn't supposed to find out about this, because if I did, I'd end it. Right?"

"That presumes," the Chorister said, "that you're the first to face the choice."

"What?"

"Every monarch has come to me," he said. "Every single one. None could resist the warning to keep out."

"I don't believe you," the princess said. Of course she'd seen the shades of the past monarchs. She knew they'd been in the Carse. But they couldn't have come this far. They *couldn't* have known about the horrors in the heart of the Carse and allowed them to continue.

Could they?

Aon stepped away from the dreadwillow. "When I first arrived, the creatures here thought I was you. They said they were expecting you. They knew you'd come."

Jeniah felt ill. Every monarch. They'd all known exactly what was going on. Even her own mother. And in the name of peace, in the name of prosperity, they'd all agreed to let the terrible ritual continue.

"Then why the warning?" Jeniah asked. "If every monarch was meant to come here, why warn us off?"

The Chorister shambled over to a tree stump and took a seat. "If your mother had brought you here, held you by the hand and explained the pact, and then beseeched you to consent and thus maintain the everlasting bliss of the Monarchy, would you have done so?"

"Without question," Jeniah said immediately.

"And *that*," the Chorister said, holding out his hands, "is the reason for the warning. This is not a decision anyone else can make for you. The warning forces you to find your own path here, and that path gives you all you need to know to make the decision."

Aon placed a hand on the princess's elbow. The anger had left her face, replaced with sad understanding.

"This is why the royal family can feel something other than happiness. It's why you're immune to the effects of the Carse."

Jeniah nodded. "The decision is too important to be made by someone who knows only happiness. The monarch has to understand pain and loss, or the choice is meaningless. But why can you feel sad, Aon?"

The girl glanced at the Chorister. "It's . . . in my blood."

Thoughts—like a swarm of angry bees—clouded Jeniah's mind. It was heartless. Why should she pay for the legacy of her ancestor? She shouldn't be the one making this choice. She was just twelve. She wrung her hands, her fingertip grazing the opal ring she wore.

No. She was Queen Ascendant. And she had a duty.

"If I consent," Jeniah said, "the Monarchy continues as it always has. If I break the pact, the Monarchy falls."

"If you break the pact," the Chorister said, "pain and sorrow will return to the land. The Monarchy, as you've always known it—as anyone alive has ever known it—will cease to be. It will be a new age. You will still be queen. But of what, I wonder? A realm of people whose joy is tainted by fears and problems? A land of plenty no more? The destruction of everything Isaar worked so hard for?"

Jeniah pictured the resulting chaos. *That's why the Monarchy keeps an army.* With the return of pain would come fear. And with fear, the potential for war. The soldiers would be needed to restore the peace.

The princess considered. The Chorister was right about one thing: she had no idea about the war that had torn the land apart all those years ago. No one did. How could she condone bringing back the possibility of war when she didn't fully understand its horrors?

"And would *you* care to advise your sovereign?" The Chorister turned and addressed Aon.

Aon started, surprised. "The princess has to choose. Why are you asking me?"

"The only way to save your father is by choosing someone to take his place. That can't happen if the princess ends the pact."

"Is it true?" Jeniah asked. "Can you save her father if I consent to the pact?"

"For an exchange . . ." The Chorister looked meaningfully at Aon. The girl bowed her head. She wasn't about to say a word.

Jeniah weighed her options. She could agree and

allow her subjects to continue living in a gilded paradise. And it would almost certainly mean that the guilt of allowing those four people every year to become dreadwillows would eat at her, as it did her mother. And her grandmother before. And nearly every monarch in the family line.

But this wasn't about what it would do to her. It was about the Monarchy. The Chorister was offering exactly what she'd always wanted: to be loved as the monarch who kept the peace. She could have magic *and* be a great ruler. The price seemed small in comparison to the gain. A queen should be willing to make sacrifices for the good of her people. Shouldn't she?

Overhead, a faint caw pierced the silence. Jeniah looked up. A falcon soared high above the trees, chasing a flash of red in the dim light. A rubywing.

Yes. She needed to make a sacrifice for her people. *All* her people.

Jeniah made her decision. She turned to face the Crimson Hoods.

"I am Jeniah, Queen Ascendant of the Monarchy. My family has ruled this land since the very highest mountains were mere pebbles. You were set this task by my ancestors—each renewing the bond as the

Monarchy changed hands—and you have done your duties faithfully and served your monarchs well. But that ends here and now with me. I dismiss you."

The Crimson Hoods stood impassively for so long that Jeniah began to suspect they hadn't heard her. Or they were being disobedient. Then, without a word, without so much as a gesture, they both turned on their heels and walked away. As they marched deeper into the Carse, the mire rose up to swallow them slowly. The mists curled around their robes like a final embrace. Soon, they were gone.

The air rent with a sound like a great curtain tearing. White and orange sparks burst up out of the briar, racing along and igniting every branch and thorn, until the entire wall surrounding the heart of the Carse was consumed with fire. Like all the other magic Jeniah had witnessed in the Carse, the flames were thoroughly destructive. They twisted and danced until, all at once, the briar crumbled to a cloud of ash. The fire vanished as quickly as it had risen. When the cloud had cleared, Jeniah looked around.

"And as for you, Chorister . . ."

But the Chorister was nowhere to be seen.

Chapter Twenty-four

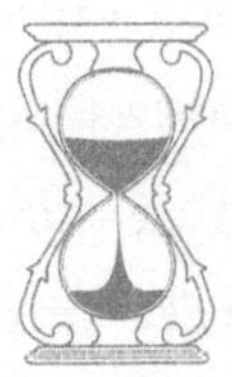

THE SUN HAD JUST STARTED TO RISE ON EMBERFELL WHEN AON and Jeniah emerged from the Carse. They hadn't spoken a word to each other on the trip out. The silence itself said all that needed saying.

Aon couldn't stop staring at her hands. They'd returned to normal, as had the rest of her, when Jeniah broke the Carse's power. But even though she was no longer changing, she couldn't shake the feeling that there was still an imp inside her. She liked the idea.

"Are you angry with me?" Jeniah's words came out in a nervous rush.

"Angry? No."

"But you were."

Aon chose her words carefully. "I was angry with your family. But they thought they were doing what was best: sacrificing a small number so many more would be happy. And when the Chorister offered me a similar choice, I couldn't make a decision at all. You made a brave choice. I don't know how you did it."

"That's the decision I made *today*," Jeniah said. "Yesterday, I may have chosen differently. I can't stop thinking that if I'd agreed to the bargain, I could have saved your father."

"But then someone else would have to be chosen," Aon said. "I'd like to believe that if my father weren't under the influence of the Carse, he would never allow someone else to suffer for his own freedom."

Jeniah shook her head. "There's not always going to be one, true answer. I guess I'll have to get used to that."

They paused on the corner of Emberfell's town square. Aon could have lain right there on the baker's front stoop and fallen asleep. Exhaustion pulled at her more strongly than the Carse's heaviness ever had. But first, she had work to do.

"Your Highness . . . Jeniah, the dreadwillows fed on the Monarchy's misery. Without it, they'll die out. It might not happen for a while—trees are stubborn and can live a long time—but they'll need someone to ease their pain now that the Chorister is gone. I'd like that to be me."

Jeniah smiled. "I think that's an excellent idea. But the Carse is very big."

"The Chorister said the oldest trees aren't people anymore. I only need to care for the ones in the heart. Like Father. And then there are Pirep and Tali."

"Then, as my second royal proclamation, I name you the Monarchy's Caretaker. You will have everything you need to tend the Carse. Ease their suffering, Aon, in any way you can. It won't make up for what's been allowed to go on there all these years . . ."

"But it means a lot," Aon said. "Thank you. If you hadn't sent me into the Carse, I would never have found my father."

The princess lowered her eyes. "Aon—" she started.

But Aon held up her hand. "I'll be okay. The Grand wyns are very nice. Or at least they were. Now that they can feel something more than happiness, who knows what they'll be like? But I'm sure we'll get along fine."

"When I'm queen," Jeniah said, "I'll send scouts to explore the lands beyond the Monarchy, looking for your mother."

It hurt Aon to think about her mother alone, so far

away from her loved ones. She prayed her mother had found some sort of peace.

"When they find her," Jeniah continued, "they'll say how the Monarchy has changed. And they'll tell of the important role *you* played in that change. She'll come back for you, Aon."

That single thought replenished all the hope the Carse had siphoned from Aon. She imagined her mother back at the forge in the barn. They would stand side by side, blowing hourglasses and vases and sculptures. Maybe Mother would help her tend Father's tree. Or maybe the Carse would be long gone by then, no longer able to feed off misery. There was no telling how long it would take to find her mother, after all. But knowing Jeniah would stop at nothing to find Mother convinced Aon that it *would* happen. Someday.

Slowly, people emerged from their houses. They made their way to work, greeting one another with a nod. Merchants swept away the cobwebs from their windows. To Aon, it all looked like the same Emberfell. But she knew it wasn't and would never be again.

"I wonder what it's going to be like," Aon said, surveying the town. "To wake up with emotions you never experienced. It would be like having a new sense."

"Or maybe just learning who you really are," Jeniah said.

I know now who I really am and who I can never be. Aon's mother's words returned like a long-lost echo, and Aon understood them at last. Her mother could never be the kind of person to accept what was happening in the Carse.

"It's not going to be easy," Aon said. "You heard the Chorister: 'Pain and sorrow will return to the land.'"

"But the joy will be there, too. They get it all. The good, the bad . . . People will return to what they were always meant to be. People will be like you, Aon."

Aon laughed. It felt good. "Are you sure that's a good thing?"

Jeniah took her friend's hand. "You're the reason I broke the pact, Aon."

"What do you mean?"

"People are *supposed* to feel sad. They're supposed to get angry. Being happy all the time . . . It isn't real. But you . . . You're real. And you're wonderful. You have to know fear to be brave. And I think you're the bravest person I've ever met. The Monarchy needs more people like you."

Aon had never thought of herself as brave. Of all

the feelings she'd hidden away from the people around her, courage was something she'd never considered.

Jeniah hugged Aon. The two friends stood there, letting silence speak for their hearts.

Then Aon stepped back and bowed low. Jeniah giggled and nodded regally. Eyes connected, they backed away from each other slowly, neither wanting to be the first to turn and face this strange, new Monarchy without the other. Finally, the princess squared her shoulders and wove her way through the growing crowd on the street, on her way back to Nine Towers.

"Constable!"

The shrill cry from up the street made people nearby jump in surprise. Aon turned to see Laius, still in his nightshirt, running barefoot down the cobblestone. His familiar, friendly smile was gone. Now, his brow was furrowed, and a look of sheer terror twisted his face.

Just before Laius reached the constable's door, he caught sight of Aon and stopped. Aon waved at him. The boy looked dumbstruck. Then he turned and barreled straight at his adopted sister, nearly knocking her over with a powerful hug.

"You're safe!" he cried. "The princess found you.

I'm so glad. When I woke up this morning and realized you weren't home, I was . . . I was . . ."

"'Worried,'" Aon said, teaching him one of Mother's secret words. Well, secret no longer. "You were worried. Thank you, Laius."

"What happened to you in there?" he demanded. He suddenly seemed quite cross that Aon had worried him. And she loved that.

"I've been to the heart of the Carse," she announced. "In fact, the princess has placed me in charge of its care. And I'm going to need your help."

"Me?"

"Yes. Forget about glassblowing. I need your natural talents. Listen." Aon hummed the strange waltz that the Chorister sang to ease the dreadwillows' pain. The boy nodded, and then he repeated the tune back with his glorious singing voice. "Perfect."

"How will my singing help?" Laius asked.

"Let's go home," she said, taking his arm. "I'll explain there."

Together, they walked back. Aon took a deep breath of air filled with the scents of the baker's scones and hay from the nearby livery stable. Something about this morning seemed more . . . in focus than any other. She felt like she'd finally wiped away a haze through which she'd been seeing life all these years. The reds on the fall leaves now glowed like hot coals. The droning chatter of the villagers starting the day changed to a glorious symphony of voices: happy, sad, and everything in between.

The princess was right. Nothing would be the same. And that was a good thing. This new world came with new feelings. For Aon, they were emotions she'd felt for a long, long time. But even Aon found herself feeling something brand-new.

I'm not broken.

The words pulsed in Aon's head, foreign and peculiar. Like some ancient tongue that had lost all meaning. And at the same time, they radiated within, thawing all that remained of the Carse's frigid heaviness.

I'm not broken, and I never have been.

Chapter Twenty-five

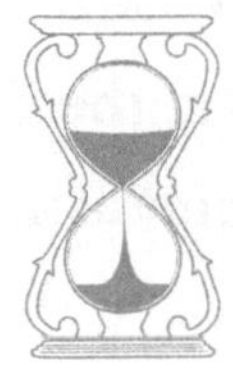

JENIAH CONTINUED TO WATCH THE SUNRISE FROM THE BALCONY in her bedroom. She ached for sleep, but she *had* to see it. The rest of the Monarchy, much like Emberfell, looked unaffected by what had happened in the Carse. Great volcanoes hadn't erupted. Monsters hadn't crawled up over the mountains and devoured the towns and villages. The Monarchy had not fallen.

And yet, it had. Everything that had made the Monarchy work for a thousand years was gone. The warning had been right after all. But something new would rise from this fall. Jeniah swore to that. It really was a very different place. *And maybe*, the princess thought, *it's time for a very different kind of queen.*

The door to Jeniah's bedroom flew open, slamming into the wall with the sound of a cannon's report. Jeniah glanced over her shoulder to find Skonas storming in, a great sack slung over one shoulder, Gerheart, the falcon, on the other. When he spotted her, he grunted and overturned the sack. Mounds of books fell to the floor.

"Well," the tutor said scornfully, "it seems we have some work to do. The healers assure me your mother doesn't have much time left. You need to learn to be queen and soon. And since you refuse to set the fourth lesson, we'll resort to these books. You like books? Well, grand! Start with that red one. It tells you all about diplomacy. Very dry and boring. Not unlike you."

It was as if the conversation they'd shared in the servants' tower was nothing more than a dream. Gone was his earlier kindness. This was again the Skonas she first knew: mercurial, cold, and demanding.

Jeniah forgot her fatigue. "How dare you! You have had more than ample time to teach me. Instead, you did nothing. You sat by, wasting time you knew my mother didn't have."

"*You* wasted that time," Skonas snapped back. "What

thanks did I get for the help I gave? None. No thanks at all from the spoiled princess. You want to be a great queen? I don't see how that can happen until you learn to stop thinking solely of yourself."

"I've been thinking of the people of this Monarchy," she said. "In fact, I—"

"You *risked* the Monarchy. You knew the dangers of going into the Carse, but you went anyway."

For a moment, Jeniah was stunned. How did he know what she'd done? No one but Aon and Laius could possibly . . . And then she realized.

"You knew I would go to the Carse," she said. "From the day you met me, you knew."

"Of course I knew. My every moment in your presence has been spent preparing you for it. And what good did it do? You never set the fourth lesson. And you never will. You don't have it in you. The princess who burns with a thousand questions! You will never be more than thc sum of your curiosities."

Jeniah could hold her rage in no longer. "And I'm proud of that! My curiosities are the very best of me. They keep me exploring. My curiosities led me to understand that Isaar had chosen poorly."

Jeniah's words shot out in fast, furious bursts. Her temples ached. She glared at her tutor.

"You told me I was my own best teacher, but I needed the guidance of others. You told me I could trust only what I'd seen and heard myself. But the shades in the Carse showed me I couldn't even trust that, because some things are not what they appear to be. You taught me that helping more people was better than helping a few. But I've seen what happens when one person knowingly suffers so many can thrive, and it made me sick. It was wrong. It was all wrong! The only thing I know for sure about being a queen is that I need to *question everything*!"

Skonas pursed his lips. Jeniah waited for his retort, but he didn't speak. He seemed unable.

Then a slow, slick grin arced above his chin. Tight and lipless, but also wide and knowing. His eyes lit up with something there was no mistaking: pride.

"You know all you need to rule," he said, turning to go. Then he stopped and added, "Your *Majesty*." As he left, he hummed that same tune she had always heard him singing everywhere he went.

A sad, haunting waltz.

It was time.

The Chief Healer collected Jeniah and brought her to the queen's bedchambers. The first thing Jeniah did was open the curtains to let the sun in. The queen would want to see the Monarchy once more. As sunlight filled the room, Jeniah slid into the bed and lay next to her mother.

"You lied," Jeniah said. She wasn't angry. She wasn't hurt. She was merely looking for answers. "About the Crimson Hoods. About the Carse. About everything."

The queen drew a long, rattling breath and didn't respond for quite some time. When she did, she said, "Parents only ever lie to their children to protect them." Then she sighed. "I have yet to see it actually work."

Jeniah took her mother's hand. It burned hotter than ever.

Queen Sula wheezed. "Forgive your foolish mother who thought she could spare you from it all. Tell me what happened."

Jeniah confessed everything: her deal with Aon, how she'd risked the warning to save her friend, and how she'd ended the pact with the Chorister. She told her mother all about Aon, how the girl would be tending to the Carse and how Jeniah planned to send a party to search for Aon's mother, the woman who left because she'd learned the cost of the Monarchy's happiness and refused to be part of it.

Jeniah stopped when she spotted tears swimming below the queen's eyelids.

"I never wanted you to find out," the queen said, her voice cracking. "My mother didn't want me to find out. Every monarch, since Isaar, has passed on that warning and prayed their children would finally be the ones to heed it."

"But I needed to know."

"If you never knew, then the guilt could never eat at you. You would live a good long life. I tried so hard to keep you from that cursed place."

"Because you didn't want me to face the choice."

The queen nodded. "And because I didn't want you to know what I had chosen. I'm ashamed I allowed the pact to continue. At any time, I could have returned and ended it. But my people were content. And they thanked me for that. I put my desire to be loved by the people above my duty to see that all are protected.

"But you, my dear sweet Jeniah, knew better. I am so very proud. You have righted an ancient wrong."

"I only did what I thought you would want me to do," Jeniah admitted.

"You were brave, doing what I could not. What no monarch before you could do. You will be the best queen the land has ever seen."

Jeniah moved closer to her mother and laid her head on the queen's shoulder. Her mother had been encouraging her for a long time, telling her she had what it took to be a good queen. For the first time, Jeniah suspected that might actually be true.

"I'm still afraid, Mother," the princess said quietly.

"That makes two of us," the queen said. "Maybe, just maybe, if you hold my hand, we can both find the courage we need for what comes next."

And they sat quietly, the queen and the Queen Ascendant. They fended off the autumn cold with love, spoken and unspoken. They watched the sun hit its zenith. Hands held tight, they shared all the courage both would ever need.

As twilight embraced the Monarchy, Jeniah left the bedchambers alone. She slid the second opal onto her finger, reuniting the twin rings. She was still afraid. She still had no idea what lay in store for her reign. There were many questions left to answer.

And she wouldn't have it any other way.

ACKNOWLEDGMENTS

WE'VE NEVER MET BUT I'M INDEBTED TO URSULA LE GUIN, whose work and spirit have been an inspiration.

I owe so much to Elise Howard, Krestyna Lypen, and the team at Algonquin Young Readers. Thank you for the intelligent feedback and the unyielding support.

Many thanks to Charlotte Sullivan, Michèle Campbell, and Carolyn Livingston, amazing beta readers who provided invaluable input.

Fist bumps to my agent, Robert Guinsler, and everyone at Sterling Lord Literistic.

And, as always, thanks to Benji, who provided guidance, laughter, and sanity . . . Mainly that last thing.

Brian Farrey is the author of the Vengekeep Prophecies series and the Stonewall Honor Book *With or Without You*. He knows more than he probably should about *Doctor Who*. He lives in Edina, Minnesota, with his husband and their cat, Meowzebub. You can find him online at brianfarreybooks.com or on Twitter: @BrianFarrey.